FOCUS ON LOVE

FOCUS ON LOVE

"Fall's my favorite season," Matt said.

"Mine, too."

"It is?" He grinned at me. "Then we have even more in common than I thought."

Surprised, I asked, "You think we have a lot in common?"

"No offense. I know you think I'm only a jock, but—"

"Now, hold it right there," I said. "I don't know why you keep saying that as if I hold it against you."

"Don't you?"

"No! Why should I? Being good in sports is a gift like anything else. Besides, you're good at lots of other things, too."

We grinned at each other. For the first time I felt really at ease with him. And then the realization hit me. I was falling in love with Matt Boynton! I was stunned. There had to be some mistake. I had always been proud of being an individual, yet the very first time I fell in love, it was with a guy every other girl in school was crazy about!

Bantam titles in the Sweet Dreams series. Ask your bookseller for any of the following titles you have missed:

15. THINKING OF YOU
16. HOW DO YOU SAY GOODBYE?
21. ALL'S FAIR IN LOVE
31. TOO CLOSE FOR COMFORT
32. DAYDREAMER
162. TRADING HEARTS
163. MY DREAM GUY
166. THREE'S A CROWD
167. WORKING AT LOVE
168. DREAM DATE
169. GOLDEN GIRL
170. ROCK 'N' ROLL SWEETHEART
174. LOVE ON STRIKE
177. THE TRUTH ABOUT LOVE
178. PROJECT BOYFRIEND
179. RACING HEARTS
180. OPPOSITES ATTRACT
181. TIME OUT FOR LOVE
182. DOWN WITH LOVE
183. THE REAL THING
184. TOO GOOD TO BE TRUE
185. FOCUS ON LOVE
186. THAT CERTAIN FEELING
187. FAIR WEATHER LOVE
188. PLAY ME A LOVE SONG
189. CHEATING HEART
190. ALMOST PERFECT
192. THE CINDERELLA GAME
193. LOVE ON THE UPBEAT
194. LUCKY IN LOVE
195. COMEDY OF ERRORS
196. CLASHING HEARTS
197. THE NEWS IS LOVE
198. PARTNERS IN LOVE
201. HIS AND HERS
202. LOVE ON WHEELS
203. LESSONS IN LOVE
204. PICTURE PERFECT ROMANCE
205. COWBOY KISSES
206. MOONLIGHT MELODY

Sweet Dreams

FOCUS ON LOVE

Mandy Anson

BANTAM BOOKS
NEW YORK • TORONTO • LONDON • SYDNEY • AUCKLAND

FOCUS ON LOVE

A BANTAM BOOK 0 553 29290 0

First publication in Great Britain

PRINTING HISTORY
Bantam edition published 1992
Bantam edition reprinted 1995

Cover photo by Pat Hill

Bantam Books are published by Transworld Publishers Ltd, 61–63 Uxbridge Road, Ealing, London W5 5SA, in Australia by Transworld Publishers (Australia) Pty Ltd, 15–25 Helles Avenue, Moorebank, NSW 2170, and in New Zealand by Transworld Publishers (NZ) Ltd, 3 William Pickering Drive, Albany, Auckland.

Printed and bound in Great Britain by Cox & Wyman Ltd, Reading, Berkshire.

Chapter One

I read somewhere once that you should be careful what you wish for, because you may get it . . . and boy! Whoever that was—some philosopher, or maybe my mom—was right on target.

Not that what I wished for was something outrageous, like winning the lottery, or becoming Queen of the May Prom, or even living happily ever after. All I wanted was . . . well, I'd better start at the beginning.

It was a Saturday afternoon in late October. I was standing in the middle of my room, trying to check myself out in the full-length mirror on the closet door, but it was the wrong place to stand to be able to see anything. Actually, it was the only place I *could* stand since just about every piece of clothing I owned was thrown everywhere else.

You guessed it, I didn't know what to wear. I *never* knew what to wear, and my best friend, Judy Abrams, was coming over any minute.

Leaning to the left, I looked myself over. The outfit was okay. My face wasn't too bad, either—pale skin with a few freckles, large brown eyes, and shiny brown hair. Just then, I heard a commotion downstairs. It sounded like a herd of elephants was coming up the stairs. It was Judy, of course—she's small, but she makes a lot of noise!

"Good grief, Tiff, what in the world have you got on?"

Now, maybe someone else would be offended at Judy's lack of tact. But not me. I know she has my best interests at heart and I know how much she cares about me—she just hates the way I dress. So I replied with admirable restraint, "Don't you ever knock?"

"Come on, Tiffany, just because you're having a clothing fit, don't take it out on me." She waded through all the stuff on the floor and plopped onto the bed. "Just what do you call what you're wearing?"

"I call it quiet good taste," I told her loftily, and it was. I kicked through the mess on the floor and took a good look at my outfit in the mirror. True, it was conservative—maybe even dowdy by Judy's standards—but what's wrong with a nice beige cable-knit sweater over a knee-length beige-and-brown-checked skirt? Everything, I knew. Who was I kidding? I looked like someone going to tea with her grandmother. Don't get me wrong, I love my grandma. But I certainly didn't look funky or cool or anything like that.

When Judy had finished giggling, she said, "I thought we were going to the five o'clock movie and then out for a burger! I didn't realize you were planning on entering the Miss Preppy competition."

I sighed. "No, huh?"

"Definitely, no. It's like you're wearing a disguise. You don't have anything to be ashamed of."

"Oh, yeah? Saturday night, two girls out on the town with *each other*? This outfit will be fine, once I find a mask to put over my face." This time she only laughed a little.

Then I noticed *her* outfit. Now, you have

to understand that my friend Judy knows what's what about clothes. She was wearing a sweat suit that didn't match—the pants with the top, I mean. The top was green with a detachable hood, and across the front was printed: SO WHAT? The blue sweatpants were patterned with yellow running stick figures, and what made it all come together were the shoes—a pair of green high-tops with neon yellow laces.

But the real reason Judy always looked good was because she is a small, cute, round, blond person—unlike me. "You, on the other hand, look great," I said gracefully.

"Thanks," she said, then added, "but who cares? I mean it. We're a couple of relaxed chicks going out together because we enjoy each other's company, not because we don't have anything better to do, right?"

"Wrong," I said as I took off the skirt, picked up a black miniskirt off the floor and pulled it on over my low-heeled pumps and panty hose.

"No," Judy said. "For starters, put on a pair of leggings. The ones on the floor in the corner'll be fine."

When she finished dictating, I was wearing an orange tank top under my father's ancient green-and-brown-checked shirt which was longish in the sleeves, biggish in the shoulders, and rather wide everywhere else. But the black leggings kind of tied it together. The leggings and the lace-up work boots, that is.

Checking my reflection in the mirror again, I decided that Grandma wouldn't recognize me if she met me on the street. But that was okay. In fact, I kind of liked it. Even my hair looked livelier.

"C'mon, gorgeous," Judy said. "Let's hit the road!"

The movie was great, an old Woody Allen flick that had everyone in the theater laughing from beginning to end. I've seen all of his comedies a million times, and I always laugh. He's my idol. Judy's, too. That's the thing about being best friends; you're alike when it counts, and *not* alike when it counts, if you know what I mean.

After the movie, we walked over to the Burger Bin. I was naming the constellations just appearing in the intense blue sky of early evening, and suddenly I almost tripped over Judy, who has this terrible habit of suddenly stopping when a thought occurs to her.

"Sorry," she said. "But see? You're having a good time."

"So?" I said, regaining my balance.

"You were so sure it would be awful to be out on a Saturday night without a date."

"I'm *always* without a date on Saturday night," I told her, "but I'm usually not *out*. There's a difference."

"Yeah. But so far it's not bad."

I grinned down at her. "Not so far, but I'm not saying things couldn't be better. What's the big deal about Saturday night, anyway? It's only one out of seven, right?"

Judy nodded. "You got it. I'm glad you finally discovered that. Roger and I have been after you for forever to come with us when we go out on Saturday nights."

"Surely not that long. And that's totally different. Third wheelies is not my thing."

"Tiffany Welles! Roger and I are practically an old married couple. You couldn't be a third wheel!"

"Judith Abrams! I don't want to go into that again." And I didn't. Yes, she and Roger had been going steady for so long that they *were* like an old married couple, but I wasn't their child. And being a third party on a Saturday night date would just be too uncomfortable for me. It was one thing when I used to hang around with the two of them on school nights, but on the weekends? It was unthinkable before Roger went off to college last month, and doubly unthinkable now that he was only home on occasional weekends.

"But—" Judy began.

"No!" I said forcefully.

"I was only going to say that you don't know who you could run into on a Saturday night."

"I'm sorry, but no one appeals."

" 'No one appeals,' " she said, mimicking me. "Face it, Tiff. You're turning into an intellectual snob."

"What?" I stopped walking and fixed her with what I hoped was a withering glance. I guess it wasn't, because she giggled.

"Just kidding. But you *do* have impossibly high standards. Who could possibly come *up* to your expectations . . . no pun intended!"

She said that because I'm tall. Five feet eleven inches these days isn't such a big deal, but it is when you're sixteen and boys your age are still a little retarded in the growth department.

The Burger Bin was jumping, as it always

was on Saturday nights. The old-fashioned jukebox in the far corner was blasting out some oldie-but-goodie, and a bunch of kids were snaking around the tables trying to dance.

"Judy, maybe we can go someplace else?" I yelled over the din. "It's so *loud*!"

"Come on! Honestly, Tiff, read my chest!" And she turned to me so I could see her motto once again: SO WHAT?

"Loud and clear," I said. We made our way through the crowd over to one of the tiny marble-topped tables along the wall. "Just remember our story—my boyfriend Pete is studying for exams along with Roger at Carlton University."

"Sure, sure," Judy mumbled, immediately burying herself in the four-page menu.

I glared at her. "Judy! You promised."

She put the menu down and gave me the benefit of her big baby-blues. "Don't worry, a promise is a promise. But when are you going to give up ol' Phantom Pete and grow up?"

"When I have to. And not a moment before." Then I buried myself in *my* menu. She was right again. It was sort of stupid, pretending I had a steady boyfriend at an out-of-town college, just because I didn't have one here—or anywhere else, for that matter.

Now, I'm not the kind of person who thinks going steady is the be-all and end-all of existence. I know better than that. I know there are other things in life, like learning about the world and life itself and people.

Usually it was okay, not having a boyfriend, I mean. But sometimes I felt kind of left out, and that's why I had invented Phantom Pete. I knew Judy understood, deep down. But she and Roger had been dating so long that she sometimes forgot what it was like not to be part of a couple.

"What're you going to have?" she asked.

"I don't know yet. It's always so hard to decide here." And it was, with four full pages of burgers, other sandwiches, and side dishes, not to mention sodas, ice cream, and exotic yogurt drinks. "I'm so hungry, I could eat the food stains on the menu," I added.

"What'll you girls have?" a waiter's voice asked. I mumbled into my menu that I wasn't ready yet, and heard Judy start to answer, then pause.

"Tiff," she said in a kind of peculiar voice. I looked across the little table at her. Her eyes were rolling wildly around, sending me a signal to look up—and up.

Standing there waiting to take our order was a tall—and I mean *tall*—killer-handsome guy I'd never seen before. Dark eyes, thick black hair, a Burt Reynolds mouth, and a dimple in his chin like John Travolta's. Wow!

"Hi, Matt," she said, stopping the eye-rolling. "I didn't know you worked here."

"Hey, Judy," the guy said. "I didn't even see you. It's so busy tonight and I'm so new here that I don't have time to look up from this order book. How are you?"

She beamed. "Just fine."

"Where's Roger tonight?"

"Exams—" I kicked her under the table. "Ouch! I mean, studying with a friend of his . . . of Tiff's. I mean, Tiffany's boyfriend, her really *steady* boyfriend, and Roger are studying together for exams . . . uh, you two know each other, don't you?"

He looked down at me. What eyes! Black-lashed and cocoa-brown. "Nope," he said.

"Oh. Well then, this is my best friend, Tiffany Welles. Tiff, this is Matt Boynton."

The indifference I saw in those heavenly eyes looking down at me turned me right back to my menu. "Hi," I said into it.

"So what'll it be?" Matt asked. His voice matched his eyes, dark and rich. I couldn't care less, I told myself.

"I'm gonna maybe have the Surprise Burger," Judy said. "What is it?"

"That's the surprise," Matt said. They both laughed. I didn't. "Actually, it's got a pineapple slice and grapes," he confided in a stage whisper. "Used to be called the Hawaiian, but it didn't sell so they renamed it. There's a sucker born every minute." They laughed again.

"I'll have the pizza-burger, medium, please, a large fries well-done, and the Double Dip Yogurt Fantasy," I said.

"You bet," he said. "Good choice. It's my favorite chow here." *So what?* I thought.

"Really?" said Judy. "Then it must be good. I'll have the same." Matt took off for the kitchen, smoothly avoiding the dancers, the other waiters, and the milling customers. Not that I noticed. I just happened to be looking in his direction.

"Isn't he great?" Judy asked.

"At what?"

"At everything! How come you don't know who he is?"

I shrugged. "Why should I?"

"Matt's a senior. He transferred from Westwood this summer, and he and Roger used to hang out together before Rog left for C.U. Matt's already a superstar. But I forgot," she said. "You wouldn't know him since you don't go to basketball games. . . ."

"Aha." I sniffed. "A jock."

". . . or take an interest in the debating society."

"Worse—a politician."

"You *are* a snob, Tiffany! As far as you're concerned, the only things that matter are things *you're* interested in."

"Wrong. I'm interested in *everything*. You, of all people, should know that. I told you I'm going to apply to the Middletown *Bugle* for an internship as a reporter because I'm so interested in everything. What more do you want from me?"

"I want you to look around, that's what," Judy said.

I was flabbergasted. "Who was pointing out the constellations about ten minutes ago? If that's not 'looking around' . . ."

"Come on! You know what I mean. Open up. Don't be such a stick-in-the-mud. Try something new for a change."

She sounded exactly like my mom. Mom

was always saying that if I didn't watch it, I was going to grow up to be a stuffy old lady. But just because I knew what I wanted to do with my life and was trying to do it didn't make me some fuddy-duddy. "Judy," I said, "this is really annoying."

"Sorry you got annoyed," said Matt, suddenly appearing at my elbow. He was holding a big tray with our orders on it. "The kitchen's kind of backed up. That's why it took so long." He leaned over to start putting everything on the tiny table.

"Oh, no," I began to say, "I wasn't talking about the service. . . ." I lifted my arm and waved right into the tray he was lowering to the table. The tray flipped up against his chest, and the burgers and fries, followed by the yogurts, splashed all over his shirt and pants. A little of the mess even landed on his chin. "Ulp," I said.

"Ugh!" Judy said.

"Hhhhmm," Matt said, grabbing at the now-empty tray as it clanged on the floor. "You're not just annoyed, you're *furious*!"

Judy laughed, so did he. Needless to say, I didn't. I kind of hunkered down in my chair and looked around desperately for something to save me. All I saw was the millions and millions of other kids in the Bin, staring, and some few hundred thousand of them laughing. If only I could have vanished in a puff of smoke! But no such luck. Pretending to be calm, I took out my wallet. "Check, please!"

Chapter Two

I loved my sociology class, and it wasn't just because I did well in it. All cultures, primitive or advanced, were fascinating to me, and so was life right here in Middletown. That's why I wanted so much to get that internship at the *Bugle*. I wanted to uncover interesting stories about the town in an original and unusual way, which was why in my application I'd planned to suggest doing a series of essays on local people's lives from their personal points of view.

So you can imagine my reaction when Mrs. Purvis, my sociology teacher, suggested almost the very same thing as a class project the following Monday morning.

"What?" I said, louder than I'd intended.

"Really, Tiffany," Mrs. Purvis said, "weren't you listening?"

"I hope I wasn't."

Now it was Mrs. Purvis's turn to say, "What?"

The entire class, led by Judy, of course, snickered. They were all looking at me. My face burned.

"Um, I meant to say . . ."

"Yes? Speak up, please." I have this tendency to mumble when I'm embarrassed.

"I mean," I continued, firmly and loudly, "it's such a good idea—would you repeat it, please?" Whew!

"Well, thank you, Tiffany, I'm glad you approve." More laughter from my classmates. "I will not only repeat it, I'll expand on it.

"Number One: The class will divide itself into six groups of four students each.

"Number Two: Each group will describe a week in the life of any member of the student body here at Horatio High, the student to be democratically selected by the group. The group must obtain the permission of the selected student—in writing, of course.

"Number Three: Each group may choose its own manner of description—for instance, daily diary entries, a series of written essays, photojournalism, even video recordings. Any method that affords an accurate documentation of a week in a student's life is acceptable."

I sat there, thunderstruck, because that was almost the exact idea I planned to present to the *Bugle*. Of course my idea hadn't been about doing personal stories on high school students. Who wanted to read about high school students? But it was close enough to shoot down the originality of my idea. I'd have to think of something else, but it wasn't going to be easy.

"And finally," Mrs. Purvis went on, "whichever group I decide has the most interesting study will have the honor of presenting it at the next full Horatio High assembly."

"Oh, boy!" I said out loud, without meaning to.

"Was that a statement, Tiffany? Or a not-so-subtle complaint?" Mrs. Purvis asked. She was a little annoyed, I guessed.

"Neither," I said. "I was just thinking out loud."

"Then try to think more quietly, please. All right, class. You have ten minutes to form your groups."

I sat there lost in thought until I became aware of someone tapping me on the shoulder. I looked up from the ink spot I'd been staring at on the scarred desk arm. It was Judy.

"Tiffany, you're with us, okay?" she said, all smiles.

"Who's us?" I asked suspiciously.

She gestured with her thumb. Behind her stood Melanie Roebuck, who is awfully pretty but a real airhead, and Walt "I'm Spock" Egremont, *Star Trek* addict, computer games maniac, and world-class geek.

I went back to staring at the ink spot.

"How *could* you, Judy?" I wailed, as we struggled through the crowded halls when school let out.

"What do you mean?"

She'd apparently forgotten what had happened in sociology and since this was the first chance we'd had to talk during the rest of the school day, I reminded her. She still didn't get it.

"What's wrong with our group? I did it on purpose."

"You *what*? Why?"

"Because now we can control the project, make it great by doing it the way we want."

"But it's supposed to be a group effort," I pointed out.

"Yeah, and in our group, we're the brains. I mean, you know Melanie, and Walt hasn't set a foot on planet Earth in his entire life."

"But there are four of us. That means your vote and my vote are only half of any decision. That's not a majority."

"Don't worry," Judy said airily. "Walt has a crush on you—if that's what it is. It's hard to tell with him. Anyway, he'll do whatever you want. And Melanie's really nice when you get to know her, though there's nothing much to know, I suppose. Come on, let's get out of here."

"Arrgghh," was all I could come up with as I followed her down the outside steps.

Judy stopped suddenly, I don't know why. Maybe it was her favorite step or something. To avoid trampling her, I made a kind of dodging maneuver into the crowd of kids to my left, tripped over someone's big feet, dropped my backpack, and went sailing over the last step, landing on the grass, but not on my feet.

I sat there, wishing small people like Judy

wouldn't do things like that. She rushed over to me.

"Oh, Tiff, I'm so sorry! Are you hurt?"

"Only my pride and maybe my rear end. I'll know when I get up—*if* I can get up."

"I promise, I *promise* I'll never stop short in front of you again." Judy grabbed one arm and I pushed off with my other, the result was that we both ended up on the grass.

"The balance was off," said a familiar deep voice from overhead. "A fulcrum has to have equal force to work properly." Matt Boynton stood there, holding my backpack. "This must be yours . . . um, Tiffany. Right?"

My face was flaming. "That's the name," I muttered, grabbing the bag from him. "Thanks."

"Welcome," he said and lifted the still-giggling Judy to her feet. Then he extended a hand to me.

"No, thanks," I said. "This time since I'm in charge of the fulcrum, it'll work." I heaved myself up, none too gracefully, and found myself toe-to-toe with Matt, but not eye-to-eye. He *was* big, probably about six feet four or five.

"Say, Tiffany," he said, his breath warming my forehead, "I didn't know you were so tall."

"Life is full of little surprises, I guess," I said with what dignity I could muster, brushing the grass off the seat of my jeans.

"Tall ones, too," he said. Judy had finally stopped giggling, so he asked her, "When's Roger due back in town?"

"Friday night," she said.

"Pete coming in, too?" he asked me.

I froze. Judy froze. Time did not freeze, unfortunately. About a year seemed to pass before I could gulp out, "Ah, um, er—*no*! No, he's got a . . . a paper due. Yeah! So, no, he won't be. Coming back, that is."

"Why did you want to know?" Judy asked.

"Just thought maybe you'd all drop by the Bin Saturday night. I know what Rog thinks about C.U., but I wanted to hear someone else's opinion. Well, another time. See you," he said, and walked off.

I couldn't believe it! "Judy, how'd he know the name?"

"What name?"

"*Pete*'s name!"

Judy shrugged. "Search me."

"You didn't tell him?"

"Why should I?" She put her hands on her hips and stared at me. "Tiffany, you tell every boy you turn down for a date that it's because you're going steady with ol' Pete. It's not exactly top secret information, you know."

"Okay, maybe. But why would anyone bother to mention it to him?"

"Probably because he asked."

"Oh, get real," I said. "Why would he ask about me?"

"I don't know. Maybe he liked getting all that food dumped on his clothes. Maybe his father runs a dry cleaner's." She grinned wickedly. "Maybe he likes you."

"That's ridiculous!" I snapped. "And anyhow, *I* don't like *him*." I started for home.

Judy ran after me—she had to, since I have this automatic tendency to lope instead of walk. "Wait up!"

I slowed down.

"What're you so upset about? And how can you say you don't like him? You don't even know him."

I stopped. "I'm *not* upset! And he doesn't know me, either. And I saw the look he gave me Saturday at the Bin."

"What look?"

"When you introduced us, he looked at me like I wasn't even there. I don't want to talk about it anymore. I've got tons of chores and homework to do before supper."

"You always do it after," Judy reminded me.

"*After*, Judy, we meet with our sociology group. Remember?"

"Oh, yeah. Now I do."

"And by the way, thanks for volunteering my house for it," I said dryly.

Judy had the grace to look sheepish. "Well, you've got that great rec room with the giant TV and not one but *two* VCRs and the tape decks and . . ."

"None of which we're going to be using. This is gonna be work. Double work with the group you formed!"

Chapter Three

By the time I got home, I was wondering why I was so upset even though I'd told Judy I wasn't. I decided it was because my terrific idea for the *Bugle* had been fouled up by Mrs. Purvis's class assignment, plus the two kids Judy had put into our group, plus . . . no, Matt Boynton had absolutely nothing to do with it.

During supper I told my parents about the kids coming over later for the sociology project. They thought it was a great idea. But when I explained how I was afraid the project would mess up my application for a job at the *Bugle*, Dad, as usual, saw it in a positive light.

"Nonsense, honey," he said, putting his arm around me and getting his elbow in the mashed potatoes as he did so. "Think of it as practice. When you work up your presentation for the *Bugle*, you'll be less nervous, more sure of yourself." Mom handed him a napkin. "Any idea can become new again, as long as you do it differently from the way it was done before."

"You missed a big spot on your sleeve, dear," Mom said. She took the napkin from Dad and removed the rest of the mashed potatoes. "Your father's right, Tiffany. I always tell my little first graders that it's the effort that counts. The results are never certain. Of course, they all want to know why. But how can you explain something like that to elementary school children?"

"Or teenagers, I suppose?" I joked.

She just smiled. But Dad said, "If you need any help, honey, call on me. I'm not the company's chief troubleshooter for nothing. You'd be surprised at the complications that even the smallest glitches in an environmental coalition can cause."

"I remember some, Dad." And I did. Like the time some dope in town had bought an ostrich because he thought it would make a great watchdog—or bird. My dad had to set the rescue operation in motion and then practically had to capture the big bird himself, when it got loose. I admired his dedication, even though I couldn't help giggling when I looked at the bowl of mashed potatoes with the imprint of his elbow in it.

At eight that night Judy, Walt, Melanie, and I were assembled in the basement rec room. Mom had made me bring down sodas and fruit juice, a big hunk of my favorite cake, and a huge bowl of popcorn. I'd reminded her that it wasn't a party, it was schoolwork, but she insisted.

So there we were, the four of us, scarfing down the food and making small talk. Finally, Judy took charge. "First we've got to decide what method we want to use in presenting our person."

I cleared my throat, about to speak, when Walt spoke instead. "This being the space age, I vote for a spy satellite!"

The rest of us stared at him.

"Walt," Judy said gently, too gently for my taste, "we don't have access to a satellite."

"Right, right," he said, blushing and glancing over at me. "I get carried away sometimes. What do you think, Tiffany?"

I opened my mouth, but Melanie cut me off. "I think . . . I think I'll wait and see what everyone else has to say first." She smiled and fluffed her short reddish curls.

"Okay," said Judy, once again taking command, "what *I* think is that we hear what Tiff thinks."

"Well," I began, "we want to be accurate and fair. Nonintrusive but truthful. And above all, we've got to make it interesting, because all the other groups want their project to be chosen for the assembly, too."

"Yeah! Way to go, Tiffany," said Walt, as if I'd said something brilliant instead of obvious.

I continued, "So, I think we follow this person, each of us taking notes. Then we meet each day and write them up together, incorporating all our points of view. That way, we'll get a real sense of the person as seen through the eyes of all four of us."

This time I got no cheer from Walt. Melanie was busy picking lint off her sweater.

After a long pause, Judy said, "Gee, Tiff, that sounds like a lot of work."

"Well, reporting *is* a lot of work, if you're going to be professional," I said.

"It doesn't sound like much fun," Melanie said.

"Sociology isn't *fun*," Walt said. "Fun is computers and outer space and . . ."

"Hold it," Judy said. "Let's concentrate a minute. Tiff suggested one method that we could do. . . ."

"All that writing and reporting and stuff is really going to interfere with cheerleading practice," Melanie whined.

"Yeah, and the time machine I'm working on, come to think of it. Gee, Tiffany," said Walt, "couldn't we do something else?"

"Like what?"

"Like, like . . ." He looked around the room, and his eyes lit up when he saw the giant TV screen, the VCRs, and the shelves full of videotapes. "Like a TV program! Why not? Mrs. Purvis said that was one way we could do it. Tape. We'll videotape whoever it is. I'm a killer with a camcorder in my hands!"

"Ooh, super!" Melanie cooed. "I bet I'd be great on camera, holding the microphone, interviewing . . ."

"I bet you would, too," Walt said with an admiring glance at her.

"Yeah," said Judy, my former best friend. "My dad even has a video camera. It's really old and the sound system's shot, but we could record the sound on a separate tape deck . . ."

"Hey! Wait a minute," I pleaded. "Videotape isn't real reporting."

"Oh, no?" Melanie said. "Tell that to Ted Koppel!"

Was I surprised. I didn't think she'd know who Ted Koppel was.

My pleading was to no avail. We took a vote and it was decided three to one to use videotape. Judy then suggested we all think about who our subject should be, and we'd get together again the next night. Walt said he'd walk Melanie home, which was another surprise.

After they left, I said to Judy, "I thought you said we'd get to do it *our* way. That Melanie wouldn't care, and that Walt had a crush on me!"

"Hey, so I was wrong. Nobody's perfect. So what? Taping'll be fun. It'll be different—I mean, face it, Tiff, we've all written enough essays in our lives."

"But *real* reporting . . ." I protested.

"Tiffany, it'll *be* real reporting. You'll make it that way."

"Me? How?"

"Simple. You'll write the narration that ties

the whole thing together," Judy said. "No matter how adorable she is, Melanie standing there with a microphone, interviewing whoever it is we pick isn't going to win it for us. This video has to be professional, like a real documentary. Get it?"

I got it. Actually, it wasn't a totally terrible idea when I thought about it. I knew I could write some really good narration, and my words would be just as important as the picture. Maybe I could make a copy of the tape and send it to the *Bugle* along with the narration I was going to write. It might impress the editors more than a sample of my writing alone. In fact, it just might get me that internship after all!

Chapter Four

The next night we were again in the rec room. Only this time, instead of all of us staring at one another, Walt was staring at Melanie, and she was staring back. Will wonders never cease?

"Okay," Judy said, "who's got a suggestion for our subject?"

No one said anything. To tell you the truth, I'd been thinking all day about writing the narration for the video, not who the video would be about. After all, what did it matter? Whoever it was, the writing was what would make it interesting. So I said, "It doesn't matter much to me. Whoever the rest of you decide on will be okay."

Walt spoke up. "Well, Melanie and I were thinking . . . how about Matt Boynton?"

"*What?*" I said.

Melanie said, "He's the star of the basketball team—all the cheerleaders just *adore* him."

"And he's great on the debating team. He even drops by the computer club sometimes," Walt added. "Melanie and I think our subject ought to be a senior—"

Melanie interrupted, "And Matt's the most popular guy in the senior class. He's dreamy . . ." Walt frowned at her. "If you like older men, that is," she added, fluttering her lashes at him.

I looked at Judy, horrified. She winked at me.

"What a good idea!" she said. "We all agree on Matt, then?"

"Wait a minute!" I said. "I didn't agree."

"You said you didn't care," Walt pointed out.

"Yeah," Melanie added.

What could I say? Nothing, that's what.

After Walt and Melanie left—arm in arm, I might add—I said to Judy "How *could* you?"

"What? What did I do?" she asked, the picture of innocence.

"Matt Boynton! He's just a jock. What could be more boring?"

"You don't know that. Besides, the point is to do the best presentation, and Matt is very popular with the student body."

"But the student body is not going to be the judge. Mrs. Purvis is!"

"Oh," said Judy. "I guess I forgot that."

"You also forgot that Matt hates me."

Judy laughed. "He doesn't hate you—he hardly even *knows* you."

"He knows who spilled a million dollars worth of food on him!"

"Don't be silly. He thought it was funny, just like he thought it was funny when you landed on the grass yesterday."

"*You* thought it was funny, too."

"Well, it was. Just relax, Tiff. Don't take everything so seriously. It'll all work out."

"Sure," I muttered. My only hope was that Matt would refuse to have anything to do with our project.

"Well, I asked him," Judy said the next day when she brought her lunch tray over to the table in the cafeteria where I was sitting.

"Did he say no, I hope?" I asked eagerly.

"No. He said sure and that he was flattered."

I groaned. "Wonderful. Just wonderful."

Melanie and Walt came over to the table a few minutes later and were overjoyed when Judy told them Matt had agreed to be the subject of our video.

"When do we start?" Walt asked.

"Three-thirty at the Burger Bin," Judy said. "I've just got to go home and get the camera."

I protested. "We've got to decide on a story line first."

"No, we don't," Walt said. "We just follow Matt around and shoot the tape. Then we edit it, and add the narration after."

"What about my interviewing him?" Melanie said.

"That's easy," said Walt. "If we can use Tiffany's dad's tape machine, she'll record the interview and the narration separately, like Judy said last night, and play the sound at the same time we show the videotape. It's not the most high-tech way to do it, but hey, we go with what we've got."

"But how will I know what questions to ask?" Melanie wailed. "For the interview, I mean?"

"Tiffany'll tell you," Judy said.

"I will?" They all nodded. "I guess I will."

I'd been hoping I wouldn't have to take part in the taping, that someone else would run the audio deck for the interviews and I could just sit up in my room and write after they showed me what they'd taped that day. But now it was more complicated. "Judy, could I speak to you—*alone*?" I hissed.

"Sure. See you guys later." She and I walked over to the soda machine. "What's up?" she said innocently.

"*What's up?* You're asking me *what's up?* You know what's up!"

Judy sighed. "Tiffany, chill out, okay?"

"Look, you've corralled me into working with a couple of people I have nothing in common with on a project that was once very important to me, the present subject of which doesn't like me . . ." I began.

"Wow! You sure have a way with words!" Judy giggled. "What're you worrying about? Walt and I will take turns running the camera, you write down some questions for Melanie to ask, and then you'll record the sound. What could be simpler?"

"That's not what I'm worried about—it's having to spend an entire week hanging around Matt Boynton."

"If, as you say, he doesn't like you—which

I doubt—but anyhow, if he doesn't, then he won't talk to you and you won't have to talk to him. Simple. See you at the Bin. Get the tape recorder, make up some questions for Melanie to ask, and change your clothes." She walked away.

"Change my clothes?" I echoed, but she was out the cafeteria door.

At half-past three, the Bin was busy as always.

I got there before the others and saw Matt rushing around with various orders. Nobody was spilling anything on him, I noticed.

I'd run home and changed my clothes to something I hoped would be more acceptable to Judy—skintight jeans, a long-sleeved acid-green T-shirt, and an old vest I'd bought ages ago in a thrift shop. I'd even restyled my hair into a ponytail on the crown of my head.

I'd lugged over Dad's tape deck in a large canvas bag with a sturdy leather shoulder strap and was standing just inside the door, the big bag at my feet, waiting for Judy, Melanie, and Walt.

Matt came by with a stack of dirty dishes, and stopped when he saw me. "Hi," he said, pleasantly enough.

"Hi."

"Where's the rest of your motley crew?"

"Late."

There was a long pause.

At last, he said, "Well, always nice talking to you," and he started away. But he didn't get very far because his foot got caught in the leather strap of my bag, and he and the stack of dishes hit the floor with a crash.

What a noise! What a mess! I expected him to be furious, but instead he looked up at me with a grin and said, "Just the kind of thing a dumb jock would do, huh? You ought to see me on the basketball court!"

What could I say? I wanted to tell him I was sorry, but I was too horrified to speak. So I bent down to try and help him pick up the broken dishes. Somehow, I managed to slip on something yucky and landed on the floor beside him eye-to-eye just as Walt, Melanie, and Judy arrived.

"What a moment!" Walt said. "Too bad we couldn't get it on tape." Somebody giggled, and it wasn't me.

As Matt and I carefully, very carefully, got up from the slippery floor, he said, "Relax. With Tiffany around, there's bound to be many more such moments."

Matt went off to get a broom, and Melanie asked, "Did you do that on purpose, Tiffany?"

"Don't be silly," Judy answered. "The plan is to capture Matt on videotape, not to kill him!"

For some reason, they all found that very funny.

Trying to ignore my wounded dignity, I said, "I have the questions for your interview written down, Melanie," and handed her a yellow pad I'd taken out of the canvas bag.

"Oh," Matt said as he swept up the broken plates. "Tiffany's not the interviewer?"

"She's gonna run the tape deck," Judy told him.

"Uh-oh," he said. "She might be dangerous with a microphone in her hand." He gave me a sly, amused look out of those dark eyes, and I could hardly help smiling back.

"Okay," Judy said. "Lights, camera, *action*!" The taping of a week in the life of Matt Boynton had begun.

Everything went pretty well, all things considered. Matt worked hard in his job as a waiter. He was efficient and polite, and all the girls in the place flirted with him and giggled at his jokes. I couldn't help but notice their response since I was recording the sound.

When Melanie interviewed him, he answered every question she asked, but he was also able to make some of his answers funny—though, believe me, the questions I'd written weren't meant for laughs. Not that he ruined them by the way he answered. He just made them different, somehow, maybe even more interesting than they might have been.

But Matt didn't turn everything into a joke. For instance, when Melanie asked why he was working at the Bin, I thought he'd say for extra spending money to buy clothes, CDs, maybe even a car. But it turned out he was working to help pay his college tuition at C.U. next year. And when she asked why his family had moved to Middletown, he said very directly and without any self-consciousness that it was because his father had lost his job and thought that relocating here would be a good idea. "As a matter of fact, he was right," Matt said. "He got a position right away with the Admiral Boat Company. But then my dad is always right—*almost* always," he added with a wink.

Matt then motioned us to the kitchen. He held the door open for us to file in and as I passed him, he said, "I hope you didn't hurt yourself back there."

"Nope," I said. Then, figuring that being polite wouldn't hurt, "What about you?"

"Nope," he said in my exact tone of voice. This time I couldn't help giggling, just like the other dopey girls had been doing all afternoon.

Chapter Five

We left the Bin at five when Matt's shift was over. It turned out that he lived only a couple of blocks away from my house, so he and Judy and I wound up walking home together while Walt and Melanie went the other way.

Judy talked and talked all the way to my door. Matt listened and nodded. I kept finding myself yards ahead of them and having to stop and wait for them to catch up.

Finally, we were in front of my house. Judy said she'd come in.

"When do we three meet again?" Matt asked.

I said without thinking, " 'In thunder, lightning or in rain'?"

"Huh?" Judy asked, looking confused.

Matt and I answered in unison, *"Macbeth!"*

I looked at him in surprise. If he could quote Shakespeare, maybe he wasn't such a dumb jock after all. He gave me another of those sly glances out of his chocolate-brown eyes and walked away, whistling.

Judy ran after me into the house. "He *does* like you, Tiff. He really does!"

"Oh, come on. Anyway, how would you know? You were talking up a storm the whole time."

"I was just asking him about himself—you know, getting more background material like a good reporter."

"Right. Only he wasn't answering."

"Yes, he was. But you were always ten feet in front of us, so how could you hear?" She paused, then said, "Tiffany, are you jealous?"

"Me? Jealous? Of what?"

"Not of what. Of whom," Judy corrected.

"You mean of *you*? Why should I be?" I asked. "You're supposed to be going steady with Roger."

"I *am* going steady with Roger." She grinned from ear to ear. "You are *too* jealous! And I'm glad!"

"Some best friend you are!"

"I'm glad because it means you like him," Judy said happily.

"And what about you?"

"I'm in love with Roger, dummy, but I think Matt's a dreamboat, and just your style."

Up in my room after dinner with a pile of homework I had to get through, I found myself thinking about Matt. He wasn't at all the way I thought he'd be.

He didn't let things like dumb accidents bother him. He was at ease with all sorts of people, he had a terrific sense of humor, and he quoted Shakespeare! I reluctantly decided he was okay, and a fit subject for our sociology project. But as for what Judy said about him liking me—

Mom interrupted my thoughts by yelling up the stairs that there was a call for me. I got a big shock when I picked up the extension in the upstairs hall.

"Hi, Tiffany, it's Matt."

"Matt?" I repeated. I couldn't believe it. Why on earth was he calling me?

"Matt Boynton—you know, the guy you're determined to knock off."

I couldn't help but laugh.

"You've got a nice laugh," Matt said.

"Thank you."

"Don't thank me—it's your laugh, not mine."

I laughed again. Though my heart was racing for some reason, I wanted to sound casual, so I said, "What's up?"

"Nothing much. I just hoped we could have a truce."

"Why? Are we at war?"

He chuckled. "Not as far as I'm concerned. But I figured since we're working together on the incredibly fascinating story of my life, I'd try and find out what I've done to make you dislike me."

"But I *do* like you," I blurted out before I could stop myself.

"You do? . . . Tiffany, are you there?"

"I don't *dis*like you," I said, thinking of a million ways to die. "You seem—uh—very nice. Why wouldn't I like you? Everybody likes you, or so it seems."

"If that's a compliment, thanks—I think. I'll take what I can get. I also called to let you know we can probably finish up the taping this weekend because I won't be working at the Bin. Unless your boyfriend changed his mind and is coming in after all."

"Boyfriend?" I said stupidly.

"Yeah. His name's Pete, right?"

"Oh, right. Pete . . . No. No, his mom's sick," I babbled.

"I thought you said he had to work on a paper," Matt said, sounding puzzled.

"Yes . . . yes, that too. His mom and his . . . um, paper."

"Well, that's good. I mean, it's too bad about his mom, and that you won't be seeing him. But it's good for us. . . ."

"Huh?" What did he mean, "us"?

". . . because like I said, we can probably finish the taping then."

"Right. Right. Okay, I'll tell the group. And, um . . . tomorrow we're taping the debate in assembly."

Matt groaned. "I forgot about that. Do you have to?"

"Well, yeah. It's one of the activities you're involved in, and this is supposed to be an accurate portrayal of—"

"I know, I know. And you want to leave no stone unturned, right? It's just that this will be the first time I'll be doing the rebuttal for our team, and I might make a fool of myself."

"Oh, you couldn't!" I heard myself exclaim. What was wrong with me, anyway?

"You really think that?" he said, as if what

I thought mattered to him. "Thanks, Tiffany. That makes me feel more confident."

It did? "I'm glad. Horatio High needs a win."

"We do okay in basketball."

"Yeah, but that's different."

"Dumb jock stuff, huh?"

"I didn't mean it that way," I said hastily. "I meant, using your brain is important, too."

"I couldn't agree with you more. See you tomorrow then. Maybe afterwards we could have a soda and talk."

I gulped. "About what?"

"The taping, or any subject you choose." He laughed. "Okay?"

I gulped again. "Okay."

"And Tiffany—hazel eyes are my favorite." He hung up.

Hazel eyes? But mine were brown—plain, boring old brown. Almost in a daze, I wandered back to my room and looked in the mirror. As I stared at my reflection, I noticed that in the light from the lamp on my dressing table, my eyes really *did* look hazel. And they were filled with unanswered questions.

Chapter Six

The following day, Matt was terrific in his rebuttal, and Horatio High beat Truman High in the debate.

I didn't hear all of it since most of the time I was crawling around on the floor under the curtains at the back of the stage, trying to pick up the questions and Matt's summations and challenges on the audiotape while Walt handled the video from out front. But what I could hear impressed me a lot. Matt was smarter and quicker than any other guy on either team.

When it was over, I was standing in the wings, the microphone wires draped all over my dust-encrusted clothing and looking like something newly emerged from a vacuum cleaner.

That's how Matt found me after everyone had finished congratulating the team. "Hmmm," he said. "Is that you, Tiffany, or the Dust Ball That Ate Manhattan?"

Luckily there was so much dirt on my face that no one could see how much I was blushing.

"It's her, all right," said Judy, brushing me off, coiling up the wire, and in general acting like my mother. "She just needs to change clothes and wash up."

Matt grinned. "She looks fine to me. I like the lived-in look. How about that soda, Tiffany?"

Judy's mouth fell open, but for once, nothing came out. Meanwhile, Walt and Melanie had been busy playing the audiotape.

"Beam me up, Scotty!" Walt said. "There's definitely intelligent life down here."

"What he means," Melanie interpreted, "is that Tiffany got all the wonderful things you said on the tape, Matt."

"That's good," Matt said, "but I wouldn't say I was wonderful."

"You were twenty-first century enough to win it for us," Walt added.

"Teamwork, that's what it was," Matt said modestly.

"So's basketball," Judy said, finally able to speak, and giving me a hard stare at the same time.

"You guys are quite a team, too," Matt said. "I don't know how this thing you're doing is gonna turn out, but if I were Mrs. Purvis, I'd give you all an *A* for effort."

"Wait till you see us in action at the basketball game Friday night," Walt said. "Actually, don't pay any attention to us—just keep your eye on the ball."

"I always do," Matt said. Then he turned to me and said, "Meet you outside after school?"

I nodded, avoiding Judy's curious gaze.

What did we talk about that afternoon? It's hard to remember everything now. As it turned out, we didn't get to have a soda. We just walked and walked. It was a beautiful day, like only October days can be. The leaves were all beginning to change, the maples turning red, the willows yellow, and the sky was so blue, it almost hurt my eyes.

"Do you see how much bluer the sky looks than it does in summer?" Matt asked.

"Yeah," I said, for once at a loss for some clever comeback.

"And do you ever notice how around five or six o'clock the color becomes even more intense?"

"Yeah," I said again.

"Fall's my favorite season."

"Mine, too."

"It is?" He grinned at me. "Then we have even more in common than I thought."

Surprised, I asked, "You think we have a lot in common, Matt?"

"No offense. I know you think I'm only a jock, but—"

"Now, hold it right there," I said. "I don't know why you keep saying that as if I held it against you."

"Don't you?"

"No! Why should I? Being good in sports is a gift like anything else. Besides, you're good at lots of other things, too. You're not just a—an athlete."

We grinned at each other. For the first time I felt really at ease with him. And then the realization hit me. I was falling in love with Matt Boynton! I was stunned. There had to be some mistake. I had always been proud of being an individual, yet the very first time I fell in love, it was with a guy every other girl in school was crazy about! The feeling of ease vanished, and Matt noticed.

"What's the matter?" he asked softly.

"Nothing," I lied. "I just—I just realized we've been walking around the whole town and we haven't discussed the project yet."

"What's to discuss? As far as I can tell, you're all doing a great job."

"But you said that's what you wanted to talk about."

"That was just an excuse."

"For what?" My heart was thumping. If my face started to turn the color of the maples, I was sure I would die right there on the spot.

"To get to know you better. We got off on the wrong foot, and I felt bad about it," he said.

"Oh." So he was just being polite—nothing personal.

"I'd noticed you around school," Matt went on.

"You had?" The thumping started up again.

"Heard a lot about you, too."

"You had?" I knew I was sounding like a broken record, but now I was sure he wasn't just being polite, and I couldn't imagine what might come next.

"I heard about you and your boyfriend, Pete."

Disaster! Why had I ever made Pete up, anyway?

"I wanted to find out more about him," Matt said. "He must be really great."

I didn't know what to say, so I said nothing.

"Of course, no one's ever seen him. He's like—like a phantom."

You got it right, I thought dismally.

"Is he from around here? Actually, that's a dumb question. How else would you have met him?"

"Oh . . . traveling."

"Really? Have you done much traveling?"

I shook my head. "None."

"None?" Matt frowned, obviously perplexed. "Tiffany, I hope you don't think I'm giving you the third degree, but I just wanted to know because—" and there he stopped and kind of hung his head and kicked at the grass and looked so adorable for such a large person that I definitely knew I was in love.

"Because? . . ." I prompted over the pounding of my heart.

He raised his head, and those delicious semisweet chocolate eyes looked down into mine. Then he touched my cheek with one big hand very, very gently.

What could I do? The natural thing was to kind of smile, wasn't it? A big, wide, wonderful smile? So I did. I couldn't have stopped it if I wanted to, and I didn't want to, not at all. We stood there, just looking at each other.

"Pete?" he asked at last.

"You were right. He's a phantom," I said.

Matt's face broke into a gorgeous grin and he began to laugh. So did I.

After I'd explained why I had invented ol' Pete, Matt told me that he understood. "Sometimes white lies are easier for people to take," he said. "You were just trying not to hurt the feelings of the guys who wanted to take you out, so you told a white lie instead of saying 'no, thanks.' But you know something, Tiffany?" he added. "You shouldn't set your standards too high. We're all only human. Even people we think are pretty special can't always measure up. I mean, nobody's perfect, right?"

Naturally, I had to agree.

When we reached my door, Matt said, "We really are two of a kind, you know."

I had to think about that for a minute. Then I said, "Because we're both tall?"

He grinned. "No. Because we both hide ourselves a lot."

"*You* don't hide," I protested. "You're right out there in the middle of things—basketball, the debating society, the way you handle the people at the Bin. . . ."

"So are you. You're pretty and popular and successful in school—what I mean is that we don't show the *real* you and the *real* me to many people."

I agreed with that. "Well, should we? Does everyone in the world have to know everything about us? I'm basically kind of a private person."

"Me, too. I'm just glad you let me see the real you, and that you saw the real me."

Taking a deep breath, I confessed, "I even like the public you."

Matt smiled. "Maybe when we're older, it won't be so terrifying to let people in."

Terrifying. He was right, that's exactly what it was. "You're pretty smart," I said.

What he said next really knocked me for a loop. "Smart enough to want you to be my girl. You will be, won't you?"

"Well, Matt Boynton, you'll just have to figure that out!" And I tossed my hair dramatically, and went inside. Then I dashed to the living room window and watched him walk away. He was whistling.

I couldn't have whistled if my life depended on it. I was breathless, weak in the knees, even trembling a little. Be his girl? *Me?* Matt Boynton's girl? The first person who ever wanted me to be his girl was the first person ever whose girl I wanted to be! I was so happy . . . So why was I shaking? Because I was scared, that's why. And you would be too if out of an incredibly blue sky your deepest, most secret wish came true! Was I lucky—and nervous!

I raced into the kitchen where my mother was entertaining Judy. I guess I must have been glowing like a light bulb, because Judy asked, "What happened?"

"Did something happen, dear?" Mom said, stirring something on the stove.

"Oh, no," I said airily. "Nothing much. I just took a walk with the person we're doing the sociology report on." Judy nearly choked on the cookie she was munching.

"And who's that, dear?"

"Matt Boynton, that's who," Judy said.

"He's only the most devastating boy in the whole senior class!"

"Hmm," Mom said, raising her eyebrows, and went back to cooking supper.

Judy turned to me. "I want to talk to you," she said.

"I have to do my homework." I casually walked out of the room, then took the stairs two at a time. Judy was right behind me.

"Tiffany!" she cried. "Tell me! Tell me *everything*!" She followed me into my room and flopped down on the bed.

"Like what?"

"Ooh, I could kill you! You know what—*everything*!"

I began unpacking my backpack. I really did have a lot of assignments to complete. "Do you have as much homework as I do, Judy?" I asked, deliberately ignoring her question.

"I tell you what—if you don't spill it all right now, you're not going to *live* to do any homework ever again!"

There was a real limit to the amount of teasing Judy could tolerate, and she had reached it—I could tell by the dangerous sparkle in her blue eyes. So I broke down and told her all about my walk with Matt, and what he had said.

She was dumbfounded. "Are you putting me on?"

"Nope," I said.

"So this is the absolute truth?"

I nodded.

"Wow! I can't *believe* it!" she gasped, bouncing up and down on the bed.

Now it was my turn to get mad. "What's so hard to believe? You're the one who said Matt liked me when I thought he hated me!"

"That was different. I just didn't want you getting all paranoid."

"Paranoid! When do I get paranoid?"

"Whenever the subject of B-O-Y-S comes up."

"I do not."

"Do, too."

"Not!"

"Do! . . . Tiffany, are we eight years old or what?"

"Or what," I said, giggling.

Judy laughed, too. "Good!" she said. "This is just so great! Now we can double-date when Roger's in town. And now you've got someone to dress up for. . . ."

She had stopped bouncing on the bed, so I was able to sit on it too, and we hugged. "Oh, Judy," I sighed. "He and I are so much alike. I just never realized it before! We see things the same way, notice the same stuff, think alike . . ."

Judy smiled. "Yeah. That's the best part. Sharing things with someone who appreciates them the same way you do . . . Boy, do I miss Roger!"

"Well," I teased, "until he comes home, you can always tag along with Matt and me."

"Not a chance—I'm not gonna be a third wheel! Oh, Tiff, this is the most romantic thing I ever heard of!"

We both lay back on the bed and spent a good half hour sighing over how wonderful our guys were.

When we had recovered, we got to work on figuring out the best way to tape the basketball game, and worrying about whether Walt would be able to use the zoom on the camera, and whether we could convince him to keep Melanie's face out of the viewfinder long enough to get some really good action shots of Matt.

Judy reminded me to take the tape recorder to the game because we needed to tape the crowd noises.

"Oh no!" I said. "I forgot all about the narration! I've gotta get started writing it!"

"Not yet. First we finish the taping. Then

we look at it. Then we edit it, *then* you write it. You can't write it till you know what you're writing about."

"Yeah, I forgot this isn't fiction . . . it just feels that way," I said dreamily. "Like I'm smack in the middle of a romantic novel."

After supper, Matt called. It was such a funny conversation, filled with a lot of long pauses and sighs.

"Hi, it's Matt."

"Hi, Matt."

Pause. Sigh.

"How are you?"

"Fine. How're you?"

"Wonderful!" he said.

Pause. Sigh.

"I guess I'm wonderful, too," I murmured.

"*I* certainly think you are!"

Sigh. Pause.

"The game's tomorrow night."

"I know."

"You'll be there? I mean, I hope you'll be there . . ."

"Of course I will. We have to tape it. But even if we didn't, I wouldn't miss it for anything!"

Pause. Sigh.

"Every basket I make—if I make any, of course—will be for you."

I giggled. "What kind of basket? Rattan, willow? . . ."

"You're kidding me."

"Yes, I'm kidding you. I haven't actually gone to any games before, but I know something about basketball. After all, I believe we have to be aware of everything that goes on around us, don't you?"

"My philosophy exactly!"

Sigh. Pause.

Mom called from downstairs, "Tiffany! Homework."

"That was my mother—I've got to go."

"She sounded just like *my* mother."

"Thanks for calling."

"Now you're kidding me again. 'Bye. See you tomorrow."

"Yeah, tomorrow . . ."

The next day at school went by with a kind of halo around it. You know, like in a movie when somebody comes back from the dead? Anyway, that's how it felt. I seemed to float down the hallways, smiling at everybody I passed. The teachers' voices were like little birds cheeping. I don't remember eating lunch, but of course, considering the kind of food we get in the cafeteria, who'd bother remembering it?

As it happened, I didn't run into Matt all day, which was just as well because I was completely out of my element. What would I do? What would I say? Something casual like, "Oh, hi, nice to see you" or "I love you madly!"? I hadn't had any practice at being in love, and I knew it wasn't something I could look up in the school library under *L*.

When I mentioned my problem to Judy on our way home, she said cheerfully, "Don't worry about it. Believe me, it'll come naturally to you."

"Why would it?"

"Because, dopey, people have been falling in love for centuries, and they all figured it out."

"Yeah, I guess so. But how do you get over being tongue-tied? What do you talk about?"

"You talked to him all right on your walk yesterday, didn't you?" Judy asked.

"Yeah . . ."

"And on the phone last night?"

"Well, it was more sighing than talking."

"Sighing *is* talking when you're in love,"

Judy informed me. "It's a language all its own."

"Is that the way it was with you and Rog?" I asked.

"Yep. Still is sometimes."

"Only sometimes?"

Judy laughed. "Tiffany, when you've gotten to know someone as well as I know Rog, you have so much to talk about that there isn't time for sighing."

"Maybe I ought to have an outline of topics to refer to," I murmured. "My hands get all clammy just thinking about it. I mean, what if I say something really dumb, or just stand there staring at him like an idiot?"

"You've never been at a loss for words in all the years I've known you. Like I said, don't worry about it. I'll pick you up a little after seven, okay?"

"Okay." I started into the house, then stopped and called, "Wait, Judy!" I ran after her. "What do I wear?"

"Aha!" she said triumphantly. "You finally admit to my face, out loud for all the world to hear, that you don't really have a clue about fashion!"

"Yes, yes, I admit it. I know nothing about clothes, all right? Come on—what should I wear?"

After a long pause, she said, "I don't know."

"Judy!"

She giggled. "Just kidding. Okay, let's see. I'm picturing your wardrobe . . . Hmm. No, no, not that . . . not that either. No. No . . ."

I'd had enough. I grabbed her arm and dragged her into the house.

We made our usual commotion as we went up the stairs, and my mom called from the kitchen, "Does Judy want some cake, Tiffany?"

"In a little while, Mom, thanks," I called back. "We have to do some work first."

After Judy left an hour later, I surveyed the outfit she'd put together for me. It was neatly laid out on the bed. Since red and black are Horatio High's school colors, she had selected:

My red ribbed turtleneck sweater, the one I never wore because it was too tight; patterned black-and-red tights; and the black miniskirt she hadn't let me wear the other day.

Judy had said I could choose the shoes once I had the outfit on, and that the choice of shoes would become obvious to me. As I looked at the stuff on my bed, I sincerely doubted it.

After supper, I took what was for me a lot of pains over my makeup. Usually I never wear any, but I dutifully applied a little powder to my nose, a little blusher to my cheeks, and a lot of mascara to my lashes, which are fortunately nice and long. Then I put on some raspberry-flavored lip gloss. I brushed my hair till it crackled with electricity, and tied it behind my left ear with a bright red ribbon.

When I went downstairs to say good-bye to my parents, I fully expected them to have a fit about what I was wearing. Instead my father just said, "Have a nice time, sweetheart. Go, Horatio, go!"

And my mom said, "I like your hair like that, Tiffany. I'm glad to see you taking an interest in your appearance."

At 7:15, Judy, Melanie, Walt, and I assembled at the gym door. I'd brought the tape recorder and the microphone again, and the longest extension cord we had in the house in case the batteries gave out.

Walt insisted on checking the zoom on the camera by taping Melanie walking up and down the corridor. We could hear the noise of the crowd beginning as kids poured into the gym and climbed to their seats in the bleachers.

"Let's do it, gang," Judy said. As we pushed through the double doors into the gym, she pulled me aside and said, "Honestly, Tiff, you look great!"

The gym was filling up fast. Walt stationed himself in the fourth row of bleachers. Melanie ran over to join the other cheerleaders, while Judy and I staked out our position as close to the coach's area as we could. I put the tape recorder down beside me and held on to the mike.

"We'd better record some crowd noise, just in case," Judy said, so I turned the machine and the mike on.

"Stand up," she directed, "and hold up the mike—we need to get a kind of all-around feeling."

I did what she said. As I stood up, the crowd roared. The teams were coming onto the court, and there was Matt, trotting out with the other members of the Horatio Panthers, all dressed in red and black sweats. The Wallingford Wasps looked sick compared to our guys.

As the Panthers ran up to the bench, Matt saw me and waved. He should have looked where he was going instead, because he ran right into the coaches' table!

I sat down very fast and covered my eyes. "Did he get hurt?" I asked Judy. "I can't look!"

"Relax," she said, grinning. "He's fine. Oh, I hope Walt had the camera running! That scene will be hilarious!"

Chapter Seven

I didn't have to worry about Matt because I discovered that a lot of what happens at basketball games is falling down and bumping into other guys. Not quite as much as running up and down the court and shooting at the hoops, but still, there's a lot of falling and bumping. I figured that Matt had to be used to stuff like that by now, but I wasn't used to seeing him do it. I'm sure there's a lot of beauty in the game when you know what's going on. And it must take a lot of skill to score when you keep falling down and running into people. I guess Matt was pretty good at it, but I was so busy wincing every time somebody ran into him and cheering wildly whenever he got the ball into the basket, and turning the mike on and off at Judy's command, that I didn't have much time to figure out what the various moves meant.

At halftime, the Panthers were ahead forty to twenty-six. The two teams trotted off the court as if they'd been playing tiddledywinks instead of slamming the ball around and running and falling and bumping nonstop. I, on the other hand, was exhausted.

Judy, Walt, and I went outside to stretch our legs, and as soon as the Horatio cheerleaders had done their thing, Melanie joined us.

"What do you think?" she asked breathlessly.

I certainly wasn't going to talk about how fabulous I thought Matt was in front of her and Walt, so I just said, "Basketball's one heck of a strenuous game!"

Melanie looked at me like I was from another planet. "I wasn't talking about the game. What do you think of Matt? Isn't he divine? Aren't you thrilled that he's our subject?"

"Thrilled" didn't begin to describe it, but I didn't want her to know that. "I'll answer your questions in the order you asked, Melanie," I said. "Number one: I don't know much about basketball, but Matt seems to do more than his share of falling down, running around, and getting the ball into the basket. Number two: I wouldn't say he's exactly divine—he looks pretty human to me. And as for number three: I won't know if I'm glad he's our subject until we get the project done."

Walt said, "Come on, Tiffany! Matt's *great.* A perfect specimen of twenty-first century man, take it from me. And our project's gonna turn out *great,* too. I got some *great* tape of him making baskets."

"Great," I said, glancing over at Judy and trying not to giggle.

And then it was time for the second half.

Though I think I kept my cool pretty well during halftime, once the game was underway again, I was a wreck. Now I understood a little of what was going on out on the gym floor, but as they say, a little knowledge is a dangerous thing. I'd groan every time Matt got fouled and would have to take a free throw, until Judy explained that Matt was excellent at making baskets from what she called the free throw line.

As a matter of fact, he was excellent, period. He was all over the court—blocking, dribbling, and making shot after shot. The crowd began to chant: "Boyn-ton! Boyn-ton!" Then, almost before I knew it, the game was over. Horatio High had won! Matt was carried off on his teammates' shoulders, and I felt so proud, I thought I'd burst.

We were gathering up our equipment and checking various battery strengths when Matt came out of the locker room. His uniform was drenched in sweat, and he had a towel around his neck. I thought he looked gorgeous. "Tiffany," he called over the heads of the crowd surrounding him, "wait for me at the rear entrance, okay?"

"Sure," I called back, trying to hide my happiness from Melanie and Walt with a casual response.

Melanie eyed me suspiciously. "What's going on with you and Matt?"

"Nothing," I said. "He probably wants to talk to me about this weekend's taping."

She didn't seem satisfied with my answer. "Why doesn't he want to talk to all of us?"

Judy stepped in quickly. "Because Tiff's the one who's going to write the narration, of course."

"Well," Walt said, "let us know when we're going to finish the taping. C'mon, Melanie, there's this episode when Spock gets his ears pinned back by a Tragaan that I want you to see on my VCR." He pulled her along by the hand, but Melanie kept looking over her shoulder at me, a puzzled expression on her face.

After they'd left, Judy turned to me. "Why don't you want anybody to know about you and Matt?"

"What's to know?" I said, suddenly defensive. "So far, all there is to know about is a walk and a phone call. That's like telling people I ate breakfast!"

"Tiffany Welles, I can't *believe* you! Matt's crazy about you. Every time he made a basket, he looked right at you!"

"He did?" I could feel myself starting to glow again, but all I said was, "So what? And so what if I'm crazy about him? Does the whole world have to know?"

"I guess not," Judy said. "But it's nothing to be ashamed about, either."

"I'm *not* ashamed! It's just that—well, I just don't want people talking, at least not until there's something to talk about."

"Like what?"

"Like till we actually have a date—maybe more than one. Until then, I don't want people gossiping about us. I mean, what if it doesn't work out between Matt and me? I'd feel like a fool."

"You can't control gossip," Judy said. "It just happens."

"Well, in this case it *won't* just happen. Now, are you gonna help me get all this stuff into the bag?"

She did, and we walked out to the gym's rear entrance. I looked for Matt, but he wasn't there. I was crushed.

"See?" I said. "He obviously changed his mind and went off without me!"

Judy rolled her eyes. "He's probably still in the shower. Or would you want to go out with him in his smelly, sweaty uniform?"

She had a point. "But I'm so nervous," I told her.

"Of course you are. I understand completely. But you look terrific in that outfit, and I bet Matt thinks so, too. You have absolutely nothing to worry about."

Just then Matt came out the door. He grinned at both of us, making me go weak in the knees.

"Hi, Tiffany. Hi, Judy."

"Hi, Matt," I said. "Great game!"

"Yeah, it was," Judy said. "Listen, I gotta get home. Have fun, children." She winked at me and poked me in the ribs with her elbow. I could have died on the spot.

As she walked away, Matt shook his head and said, "Your friend Judy is something else, isn't she?"

"Yep," I said, determined to do away with her the first chance I got. And then I couldn't think of anything else to say.

Matt looked down at me. "Hey, are we back to 'yep' and 'nope'? What's the matter?"

"Nothing," I said. "I'm just—um, I have to . . ." I started to hoist the heavy bag onto my shoulder.

"Here, let me take that." Matt reached out to grab the strap, I let go, and suddenly we were holding hands as the bag fell on his foot.

That kind of broke the ice—luckily not his foot—and we went off to the Bin. Both of us kept laughing, especially when Matt pretended to limp.

The Bin was like a zoo since we'd just won the game. Everyone was excited. And when Matt and I walked in, the noise level went up about a million decibels.

The kids all cheered and flocked around Matt to congratulate him—apparently he'd been high scorer on the team for the third time in a row. I was kind of pushed aside by a bunch of adoring girls, but Matt reached out for me, and stood there talking to his admirers while holding my hand. I felt both proud and dismayed—the gossip mills would be spinning out of control!

He finally managed to get away from the crowd and led me to a table in a corner. We both ordered exactly the same things from the enormous menu. And then we just sat there, smiling at each other until our food arrived.

"I'm starved," he said, reaching for his burger.

"You should be. You used up more energy during that game than I do in a whole year," I told him.

"I didn't notice," he said. "The only thing I noticed was where you were in the stands."

I felt myself blushing. "What a nice thing to say!"

"Not nice. True. And I also noticed right away you were wearing the school colors. You surprised me—I figured you of all people wouldn't bother with something like that."

I decided not to kill Judy after all. "So you thought I'd be predictable?" I asked, pretending to frown.

"No way! Don't get me wrong. It's just that the more I know about you, the more I'm glad I do."

We didn't talk much while he polished off his hamburger. I offered him mine, since I seemed to have no appetite. He took it, and it too disappeared very quickly.

"Dessert?" he asked.

"No, thanks. I'm full," I said. Matt asked for the check and we left.

It was a beautiful fall night. The air was clear and cool, with a hint of wood smoke in it. We walked hand in hand down Willow Street to the park behind the library. Matt put his arm around my shoulders.

"There's Mars," he said, pointing up at the starry sky. I didn't tell him I knew very well where Mars was. "And that really bright one over there is Sirius." I didn't tell him I knew Sirius, too. "Sirius is a star in Canis Major."

I nodded, trying to do what I'd heard a girl was supposed to do when she was out with a guy, which was to pretend to know less than he did, though I didn't like doing it. It seemed dishonest somehow.

Matt pointed out all the constellations I knew by heart, and I pretended to be amazed by his knowledge. But he was smart enough to catch a tone in my voice that I wasn't smart enough to disguise.

"What is it?" he asked. "Does this stuff bore you?"

I couldn't pretend anymore—I cared about him too much not to be honest.

I took a breath and said to myself, *Here goes nothing.* Then I said to him, "No, not at all, Matt. I love hearing you talk about the stars because they interest me, too."

His face lit up. "Hey, that's terrific! Stargazing is kind of a hobby of mine."

"Mine, too," I admitted.

Matt's smile began to fade. "You mean I've been telling you stuff you already know?"

I nodded reluctantly.

"So why didn't you stop me?"

"Because I like listening to you, and—and besides, I thought maybe you wouldn't like the fact that I know a lot about it, too."

He took me by the shoulders and turned me to face him. "Listen, Tiffany," he said seriously, "what I like about you is your independence, your brains, and your looks, not necessarily in that order, of course. I hope you don't really think I'm the kind of guy who can't like a girl who's as smart as he is."

"Or smarter?" I teased. He stepped back. "Kidding," I said quickly. "Only kidding!"

His grin flashed pure white in the moonlight. "Who knows? Maybe you *are* smarter. What does it matter? Anyway, you don't play basketball. Or don't tell me you do?"

I laughed. "No," I said. "I'd never even been to a game before tonight, but I could tell you really are good."

Matt looked pleased. "Oh, yeah? How could you tell if it was your first time?"

"Instinct," I said. "Plus the fact that you made more baskets than anyone else. And anyone who can fall that many times and get up again without being hurt must really know what he's doing."

"Speaking of falling . . ." Matt's voice became softer, "this is the first time I've ever fallen for a girl like you."

I don't know why that both elated and disappointed me. Why should I have thought he'd never been in love before just because I hadn't? Again Matt sensed the change in me.

"What is it this time? Tiffany, you can change moods faster than I can count. Did I say something wrong?"

"Nope."

Matt sighed. "Here we go again with the 'nopes' and 'yeps.' " He gave me a little shake. "*Speak* to me."

This was definitely something I didn't want to discuss with him at the moment, so I said, "I was just thinking that when we finish the taping, it'll all be over."

"Not you and me," Matt said huskily. And then he kind of bent his head and we were kissing, just like that!

What can I say? A kiss is just a kiss? Well, it wasn't, not by a long shot. I'd been kissed once or twice before, but let's just say that this was the first time I knew without a doubt that I had been *kissed.* Matt put his arms around me and murmured into my ear, "The project'll be over, but you and I are just beginning. Isn't that right, Tiffany?"

I was so breathless that all I could say was, "Yep."

We stood there with our arms around each other for a while, then started walking again. I noticed that we took almost the same size steps. We didn't talk for a long time. Then I realized something.

"Matt, I'm going to be very busy for a while writing the narration for the video—after we do the editing, that is. And that will probably take ages."

"You mean you think you'll be too busy for anything else? Like seeing me?" he asked.

"I—I don't know," I faltered.

Matt took my hand. "Don't worry. I know something about video. I'll help with the editing, and you'll find me hanging right over your shoulder as you write. After all, this is my life we're talking about here. I've got to protect my interests, right?"

I brightened. "You will? You'll have the time?"

"I'll make the time," he said, and then he kissed me again.

Later that night, I sat in the kitchen eating a huge sandwich of leftover meat loaf. After Matt had brought me home, I'd discovered that I was ravenous. My parents had gone out with friends to a community concert downtown, and when they came in, they were surprised to see me sitting there stuffing my face.

"Didn't you go out with your friends after the game, sweetheart?" Dad asked.

"Mmmfff," I answered through a mouthful of food.

"Don't kids eat at the Bin anymore?" he asked. "Or do they just sit there listening to that awful racket they call music?"

Mom was looking at me. "Did you go to the Bin?" I nodded. "With Judy and the others?" I shook my head. She said to Dad, "She wasn't hungry when she was at the Bin."

"How do you know?" he said. "And why wouldn't she be? The burgers used to be great there. When I was a teenager, I was always starving after a game, especially when we won."

"Because Tiffany's a lot like me," Mom said, smiling. "Remember when we were first dating how I could never eat a thing?"

Dad scratched his head. "Vaguely."

"Well, I couldn't. And I would guess that Tiffany's the same way. I would also guess that she's got a boyfriend—" I could feel the blush creeping up my neck "—and that his name is Matt."

Dad stared at her. "The girl hasn't said anything except 'mmmfff,' and you know all that? Women!"

"Men," Mom said with a smirk.

I swallowed the last of my sandwich, wiped my mouth, kissed them both good night, and floated off to my room.

It's amazing, isn't it, how well your parents know you sometimes?

As I drifted off to sleep, I thought about Matt and how quickly he and I had discovered each other. *But I guess life's like that,* I said smugly to myself. *Sometimes we just luck out.*

Since this was my first experience of falling in love, naturally I had no idea just how smug I was.

Chapter Eight

I love Saturdays—a whole day with no school followed by another whole day with no school. Saturdays are better than Sundays because you can look forward to Sunday on Saturday. But on Sunday, Monday lies ahead.

Judy called early, while I was still buried in my closet, trying to decide what to wear.

"Walt and Melanie are meeting us at Matt's house at eleven."

"But I'm not dressed yet," I wailed.

"Tiff, it's only nine-thirty. Surely even *you* can dress yourself in an hour and a half."

"I guess. Only in what?"

"Whatever. Just put on what you think I'd pick out for you." Easy for her to say. "Now, to the really important stuff. How did it go last night?"

I smiled dreamily. "Fine."

" 'Fine'? That's all you're going to tell me?"

"You want the details? Okay. We walked, we talked, I came home. The end."

"That's it?"

"Oh, I forgot. We went to the Bin. Matt ate, I didn't. He ate what I didn't eat."

"Tiffany! . . ."

"Judy! . . ." I mimicked. "For heaven's sake, we're just getting to know each other. What else could've happened?"

"A kiss could have happened," Judy suggested. I didn't answer. "Tiffany?"

After a long pause, I said, "Look, you're my best friend, but if I tell you . . . well, I don't want you to gossip about me and Matt." Another longer pause. "Yes, we kissed!"

Judy squealed in delight. Then I said, "But I don't want to ruin everything by talking about it, not to anybody else, understand?"

"Yeah, okay. You're right, I guess. I just thought you'd be a little more excited."

"If I were any more excited, you'd have to tie me down!" I said with a giggle.

"That's better. Catch you later, alligator." Then she hung up and I returned to my closet.

As I was leaving the house a little before eleven, Mom looked at me quizzically. "Tiffany, has something happened to all your good clothes?"

I checked what I was wearing: A stone-washed denim jacket with a hole in one elbow over a striped shirt over a tank top, my oldest jeans, and high-top sneaks. "No. Why?" I asked innocently. But I grinned to myself. If Mom didn't approve of what I was wearing, Judy was sure to love it.

It was a beautiful morning. The leaves were getting more brilliant by the minute and there was a little nip in the air. It was great to be alive and in love, I thought as I walked the few blocks to Matt's house.

When I arrived, Walt and Matt were out in front throwing a football around. Melanie was posing against the trunk of a big oak, and Judy was taping the whole scene.

"Hi," I called.

Matt turned to greet me just as Walt threw the football and got him squarely on the back of the head. Matt fell like a stone to the ground. I screamed and ran over to him. He lay there, unmoving, eyes closed.

"Matt, Matt! Speak to me!" I wailed. I was beside myself.

He opened one eye and said weakly, "Three Hawaiian burgers coming up, and hold the lava!" The others laughed. Some joke! I tried to punch him, but he was too fast for me. He grabbed my hand and rolled into a pile of leaves, pulling me with him.

Judy was still laughing, but not hard enough to prevent her from continuing to tape it all. Matt and I were wrestling in the leaves like a pair of eight-year-olds, and the leaves were all over my hair and sticking to my clothes. Then Walt and Melanie decided to join us, whooping and throwing leaves in all directions.

Somehow we were eventually able to remember what we were supposed to be doing, and we got started with the taping.

We'd decided to tape Matt at his desk working, in the kitchen eating, and in the driveway shooting hoops. So we began up in his room.

It was funny—his room looked a lot like mine. I don't mean messy, with clothes all over the place. I mean it was cozy with lots of books, some of the same ones I had, plus a complete set of Shakespeare! His bed was in a corner like mine was, and he even had the same Beatles poster that I did hanging over his desk. I felt really comfortable up there.

The room was small, though, also like mine. So with the five of us, there was a lot of bumping into one another and "excuse me's." There was also a lot of laughing. Matt sat at his desk and actually did some of his homework while we were taping!

Melanie interrupted Matt a couple of times to ask more questions I'd scribbled down at home, and it all went smoothly.

Then we trooped down to the kitchen where Matt's mother had made lunch for all of us. We were surprised and grateful, since all that fooling around in the leaves had made us hungry. I was really starving because I had forgotten to eat breakfast, and my meat loaf sandwich was just a memory.

Mrs. Boynton was very nice. Kind of pretty, almost as pretty as my mother. But I have to admit Mrs. Boynton made better lasagna. She was almost as tall as I am, which made me like her just about immediately, and she had the same beautiful dark eyes Matt did. I would have liked to meet his father, but he was out bowling, Mrs. Boynton said.

We all pigged out on her delicious lasagna, but we didn't tape Matt eating because by the time we remembered, all the food was gone. During lunch, Judy, Walt, and Melanie teased me about the amount of lasagna I was putting away.

Matt defended me. "A hearty appetite is the sign of a warm heart," he announced with a grin at me.

Soon it was time to tape Matt shooting hoops. He made basket after basket from every angle, and then he made some shots that Walt called slam dunks. When Walt ran out of tape, he shot a few baskets and so did Melanie and Judy. When Matt suggested I try, there was no way I could refuse, so I tried—and failed. Oh, well.

Unfortunately, about the time we were finishing, Matt got an emergency call from the Bin to fill in for a few hours. Someone hadn't showed for work, so we couldn't even go for a walk together.

That evening, over at Walt's house, we began to edit. Walt's basement was set up the way you'd imagine a computer nut's would be—super high-tech. There were machines, keyboards, monitors, and blinking lights everywhere.

Walt fed the cassettes into a monster VCR, which then displayed them on a monitor that looked like a gigantic glass eye. As we watched the tapes and argued about what to keep and what to delete, he would mark the spot on the VCR's counter. He told us that we'd run it again later, while on a second VCR and monitor he could electronically splice it together, erasing what we didn't want.

All during the explanation, which was a lot more complicated than I've made it sound, I just nodded because I didn't have a clue about this sort of thing. Matt, who seemed to know a lot about it, said we should make a duplicate of all the original tapes in case something went wrong. I thought that sounded like a good idea, but Walt disagreed and so did Melanie. They said it would take forever, because we had shot so much footage. After all, Melanie pointed out, it *was* Saturday night, and she and Walt had plans. Matt volunteered to do it himself even if it took all night. I said I'd help, and Judy said she would too, at least for a while.

"Look," I said. "This is just silly. It makes sense to have another copy—this footage is priceless!" Then I blushed and went on hurriedly, "I mean the project's due by the end of next week. There's no time to shoot it again if anything happens to what we've got." After some more discussion, Walt and Melanie decided that they could change their plans just this once.

It didn't take very long to make the copy. Matt looked great on the tape—except for the times he fell down during the game, got hit in the head with the football, and things like that.

Everyone but Matt wanted to remove all the awkwardness that had been taped. He wanted to keep it in because it was what had really happened. But I agreed with the others. After all, the tape as it was made Matt look kind of like a clown sometimes, and I wanted his image to be absolutely perfect.

So we decided what stuff had to be removed, including all the dopey things Judy had taped while we were horsing around in the leaves and all the other clumsy or silly things Matt had done. We finished around midnight. Now all that needed to be done was for me to write the narration to go with the action. Simple, I thought.

Matt walked me home. Even though it was late and cold, we sat on my front porch for a little while, talking about college, and Shakespeare, and the stars.

Chapter Nine

Early the next day, I ran down to my basement and played the videotape—for continuity, I told myself. But I found I was watching it without thinking about anything except how wonderful Matt was, and how amazing it was that he wanted me to be his girlfriend.

I finally snapped out of it around midmorning, got the timing down, and started writing. It wasn't till Mom called me from the kitchen that I stopped. I'd written a lot, and I thought it was pretty good. My Uncle Lou and Aunt Missy had been invited for midday dinner, so I didn't have time to do any more that day.

Early that evening Matt called, and we talked for a long time about nothing in particular. I wasn't tongue-tied at all anymore. In fact, I was getting more and more comfortable with him. Being in love was a warm and wonderful feeling!

Monday was school, of course. Between gym and chemistry, I realized I didn't have a book I needed so I ran to my locker to get it. I was in a hurry and was half in and half out of the locker, trying to dig out the book, which was way at the back, when my jacket got caught on something behind me. Though I tried to reach around, I couldn't unsnag it.

My locker is way at the end of a row right against a jog in the wall. The space was very cramped, and now I discovered that there was no way to move. I was stuck!

I thought about calling for help, but with my head inside the locker, I knew nobody would ever hear me. I figured someone would come by any second but no one did. The bell had rung, and all the kids were in class. I was beginning to panic when I heard Matt's voice.

"Hmm. It looks to me like there's a damsel—or part of a damsel—in distress."

"Help!" I said. "It's me, Tiffany!"

He unsnagged me, chuckling all the while. By the time I emerged, my hair was a mess, my face was red, and I was more than a little mad.

"How can you laugh at me?" I asked him. "I could've *died* in there!"

"Hardly. Come on, lighten up, Tiffany. It was the *situation* that was funny, not you," he said, grinning.

"But I was *in* the situation."

"And you weren't in any danger."

"I know I'm exaggerating," I admitted. "It was just—humiliating."

"But I'm the only one who saw you."

"It's *especially* humiliating for you of all people to see me being so clumsy."

"You weren't clumsy. You didn't design these stupid sardine-can lockers. You didn't create the situation," Matt pointed out reasonably.

He was so sincere, and I knew he was right. But he obviously didn't understand about the wounding of one's dignity, not to mention pride. So I told him.

"What's that got to do with anything?" he asked. "You're just a normal human being . . . who got captured by a locker. It could happen to anyone." He was trying very hard not to laugh. I glared at him. That amused him, too.

"Tiffany, where's your sense of humor? Come on, I'll walk you to class."

"No thanks," I said stiffly. "I can find my classroom all by myself!" I stalked off, hoping I looked more dignified than I felt.

On our way home after school, Judy asked if I'd seen Matt. When I didn't answer, she looked at me. "Uh-oh. Something happened, didn't it? Something you don't want to tell me?"

"Yeah," I mumbled.

"Well? What?"

"Judy!" I glared at her. "You were right. It's something I don't want to tell you." We walked along without speaking for a few minutes until I couldn't stand it anymore. "We had a fight," I told her.

"You're kidding! A fight? Already? How could you have a fight? What about? What happened?"

"Well, I don't think Matt *knew* it was a fight," I confessed, feeling a little foolish.

"Then it wasn't a real fight."

We walked a little more. Then Judy stopped. "He hurt your feelings, right?"

I nodded. "No wonder you're my best friend. You know me like a book."

"Or a Woody Allen movie," Judy added, smiling.

"Yeah." I told her about getting stuck in the locker. "And he said . . . he said, where was my sense of humor?"

Judy shrugged. "So?"

"So maybe I don't *have* a real sense of humor . . . Do I?"

She thought about it as we started walking again. "Let's just say it's not your most developed asset when it comes to seeing something funny about yourself. Not that it's totally lacking. It just needs some work."

"What do you think I should do about it?" I asked.

"Like I keep telling you, just open up—go with the flow. Relax. You know."

We were at my house. "Sure," I said. "Go with the flow. Relax. Thanks a bunch." And I went inside.

I spent the rest of the afternoon in the basement working on the narration for the video. It seemed to be getting harder to do, and I didn't know why. But I kept taking deep breaths and plunging ahead. After all, we had a deadline to make and I didn't want to let everybody down.

The very word "deadline" gave me a little thrill. It was so . . . newspapery. Of course, for school we constantly had papers to write and they had to be in on time, so they had deadlines. But this was different. I wasn't doing it for the grade. I was doing it to show my skill at reporting.

That, I figured, was why it wasn't as easy to do as I had thought it would be. It was too important. It had to be just right, not only for my own sake, but for the rest of my team and for Matt as well.

Suddenly, it was suppertime. When Mom called down to let me know, I was relieved to get away from the video and my words.

Matt called while I was doing my homework. "How's it going?" he asked cheerfully.

"You mean the narration?"

"Sure. That and everything else. Meaning—uh—how are you?"

"Fine, thanks, and you?" My voice sounded so stiff and prissy that I could have kicked myself.

"Hmm. That sounds a little formal. Tiffany, are you all right?"

"Why wouldn't I be?"

I could hear his amusement as he said, "Well, it's not every day you're almost consumed by a locker."

"Ha, ha," I said dryly.

"So you're still upset, huh? Look, I wasn't making fun of you. I'm sorry if you thought I was. Like I said, the situation was silly—you weren't, honest. Tiffany?"

Then, for some unknown and very strange reason, I started to giggle. Matt snorted, which made me giggle more. Soon we were both laughing hard. I was picturing myself half in and half out of the locker as Matt would have seen me. It must have been a hilarious sight from his viewpoint. Only someone without a brain in her head would be mad at someone for laughing at such a predicament. So I laughed along with Matt. It felt great!

When I could speak again, I said, "You're right. It *was* silly."

"I'm awfully glad you see it my way," Matt said.

"Oh, I do, I *do*," I said. That ridiculous picture came back into my mind, and off I went into gales of laughter again.

Later, as I was falling asleep, I giggled into my pillow.

* * *

I told Judy all about it on the way to school the next morning.

She smiled and said, "Way to go, Tiff! I always knew anyone who was my best friend must have hidden depths."

"What does that mean?"

Giggling, Judy said, "Actually, I don't know! Hey, I like your outfit!"

"You do?" I glanced down at the denim overalls I was wearing over a long-sleeved purple T-shirt, and my ankle boots. "Good. It's all thanks to you."

"True," Judy said smugly.

Before I could stomp her to death, we were at school and running up the steps.

At lunch, Walt, Melanie, Judy, and I discussed the project. The others couldn't wait to read what I'd written—particularly Melanie, who would be doing the actual narration.

"It's still a little rough," I told them. "Let me work on it some more and smooth it out, and then Melanie can practice reading it tomorrow."

"The Klingons are coming in at warp speed, Captain Kirk," Walt said in his Spock voice. "We don't have any time to lose!"

"Oh, can it," Judy said. "If Tiffany needs

the time, she needs the time. We've got till Friday to hand it in, and we want it to be really good. The Klangons can wait."

"Klingons," Melanie corrected.

"Yeah," said Walt.

I didn't tell them that the real reason I wanted to wait till tomorrow was that Matt was coming by tonight to look it over. I thought he ought to read it first. After all, it was a week in his life we were showing. But after Walt and Melanie had left, I told Judy.

"Sounds reasonable to me," she said. "You want me to be there?"

"Tonight?" I said, surprised. "Why?"

"Moral support?"

"No," I laughed. "Thanks, anyway. Everything's fine between Matt and me now. He really understands me, and I understand him. Besides, he's never been over to my house before, and I thought . . ."

"Got it," she said with a wink. "Romance—ah, how well I remember it!"

"Rog coming in this weekend?" I asked.

"He'd better!"

"Great! Maybe we can go on our first double date!"

Matt arrived that night just as I was bringing out the dessert. "Timing," he said after I introduced him to my parents, "is everything."

They laughed, and I cut him an extra large piece of Mom's famous apple-rhubarb pie. Matt ate it with his eyes closed, an expression of absolute bliss on his face, and Mom beamed at him. He sure knew how to make friends fast—even with parents. I told him that as we went down to the basement.

"Well, I want them to like me since I *like* you a lot." He gave my hand a squeeze. "I didn't act pushy or anything, did I?"

That made me laugh. "Of course not! I just meant that you have such an easy manner. I wish I did."

"But you do," he said. "With me, anyway. It's just a question of not taking everything too seriously." He pulled me closer. "Do you think I'd go for a girl who was a stiff?"

My heart pounding, I murmured, "I—I guess not."

He bent down and kissed me then, and I melted. "Stiff" was definitely *not* how Matt made me feel!

When we finally came up for air, I said, "I guess maybe we ought to get to work, huh?"

Matt nodded. "Guess so."

I had set up the TV and the VCR before

supper. The narration was scribbled on a pad of yellow legal paper. "I've really worked hard on this, and I think I've got it right," I said. "But please tell me if there's anything you don't like, or if you think something ought to be changed, okay?" I was suddenly beginning to feel nervous.

"Okay."

"And don't worry about hurting my feelings. Okay?" What if he didn't like it?

"Okay."

"I mean, this is just an assignment, a class project, not life and death, right?" Then why was I so tense?

"Right."

"So should we start?"

"Tiffany . . ."

"What?"

"That's why I'm here," Matt said patiently. "Not that I'm not here also to see you, but this is work we've got to do. You want my opinion, you'll get it. Direct and honest."

"Right." I took a deep breath as I turned on the machines. "It's just that I'm a little—nervous."

He grinned. "Don't be. I won't bite. And what's there to be nervous about? It's my life, not yours."

We settled onto the old leather couch. The TV flickered into life; I zapped the VCR with its remote, and the tape started to play. I cleared my throat and began to read in my most solemn voice the script I'd written to accompany the videotape:

"Matthew Boynton, athlete and scholar, fond son and class leader, popular and diligent, toiler after school and on weekends to help pay his way in this difficult and contentious world . . ."

A couple of minutes into my reading the narration, I heard some odd muffled sounds. I looked up from the script and saw that the noise was being made by Matt. He was coughing or something into one of the pillows on the couch.

"What's the matter? Do you want some water?" I asked anxiously.

"No, thanks. Sorry," he gasped. "Something in my throat . . . it's okay now."

I went back to reading the script. ". . . Here we see Boynton at that popular dining spot, the Burger Bin, demonstrating his famed agility with a tray loaded with more food than any ordinary person could possibly carry . . ."

As I read on, the noises began again. Matt's face was beet-red—what I could see of it around the pillow.

I stood up. "I'm going to get you some water." I did, and handed him the glass.

"Th-thank—" he started to say and then broke into a howl of laughter.

I stared at him. "Matt! What's going on?"

"Tiff—Oh, Tiffany, I'm sorry—" he gasped.

"Why are you laughing? What's so funny?"

"The *script*—" He could barely talk.

"The script isn't supposed to be funny," I said. I was not smiling.

He was finally able to get it out. "I know . . ." and then he fell apart again.

Now I was getting mad. "Matthew Boynton, stop it!"

"I can't," he said, laughing even harder.

I was getting hurt on top of being mad. "You're making fun of me!"

"No—no I'm not . . ."

"Then what do you call it?" I shut the machines off and waited in icy silence for him to get control of himself. It took several minutes.

He wiped his eyes and sighed. Taking my hand, he said, "Sit down here."

I sat. But I pulled my hand away.

"First," he said, "it's funny to see yourself on tape. Have you ever watched *your*self?"

"No. Well, actually, yes. Uncle Lou tapes the family get-togethers a lot."

"Well, don't you think they're funny?"

I still wasn't smiling. "Sometimes. But mostly I'm embarrassed when I watch myself."

"You see? That's what I mean. I was embarrassed, so I laughed."

I stared at him stonily. "I don't believe you."

"It's the truth. Now let's hear the rest of the script." Giving Matt the benefit of the doubt, I turned the machines back on and continued reading. We had edited the tape down to about twenty-five minutes. The whole time, I was conscious of strangled sounds coming from Matt, but I tried to ignore them.

Finally, the tape and the script both ended simultaneously. I was proud of myself. I'd timed it perfectly. "Well?" I asked. "Any comments?"

Matt didn't speak.

I asked him, "Are you all right?"

He reached out for my hand again, but I moved away. At last he said, "Tiffany, I don't know how to say this . . ."

"You hate it."

"No, I don't hate it. How could I hate something that makes me out to be such a hero? Like—like Sir Galahad or somebody!"

I frowned. "What do you mean?"

"You've got the pictures of me, all right. I recognize myself. But the script . . ."

"What about it?" I asked when he didn't go on. "Will you please stop hedging?"

Instead of answering my questions, he said, "You know how much I care about you, Tiffany. You know I want you to be my girl—"

"You hate it," I muttered dismally.

"No! It's just not *me.* You've made me out to be like what I said . . . a hero, someone impossibly good and brave without any warts, not a real person."

My eyes filled with hot tears but I blinked them back. "You *do* hate it."

"Look, you guys cut out of the tape all my mistakes, all my—"

"Nobody wants to see mistakes," I exclaimed. "We're not doing a taped essay on *mistakes.* You're a star athlete, an *A* student . . ."

"Okay, okay." Matt took a deep breath. "But you've also written a script that glorifies me to the point of being ridiculous."

"What?" I jumped up. I felt dangerous. "*What?*" I repeated, my voice rising.

"It's so solemn. So *heavy.* I'm sorry, but it could be about the life of a funeral director!"

"What are you talking about?" I yelled. "What do you know about reporting—or writing, for that matter?"

"Now hold on a minute—" Matt began, but I wouldn't let him finish.

"No, *you* hold on! I worked very hard on this project. I didn't want to do the project on you to begin with, but I agreed because the others wanted to and I was outnumbered . . ."

"I didn't know that," Matt said quietly.

"Well, now you do. Not that it matters." I swallowed hard, determined not to cry. "I really care about you and I thought you really cared about me!"

"Tiffany, I do. Just because I don't think what you've written is—"

"Any good!"

"*Accurate,* doesn't mean—"

"Oh, yes it does. It means you don't know anything about me, about how I feel or what's really important!"

He stood up and made a grab for me which I avoided by backing into the coffee table. I was barely able to grab the glass of water before it fell to the floor. Carefully, I set it down.

"Nice recovery," he said, looking glum. "Please, Tiff, listen to me. You wanted to know what I thought . . ."

"I didn't think you were going to laugh at it!"

"I couldn't help it. The whole thing is very flattering—*too* flattering, that's all."

"That's all? That's terrible! Just terrible!" I started pacing up and down. "You're saying I can't be an unbiased reporter!"

Matt stared at me. "I am?"

"You're saying that because I care for you—*cared* for you—my heart got in the way of my brains!"

"When did I say that?"

"You didn't *say* that, but that's what you thought!" I was so angry, so hurt, that I couldn't see straight.

"I never said it and I don't think it, either. And what d'you mean, *cared* for me?"

"Past tense, that's what I mean."

"Come on, Tiffany. Over such a little thing?"

"Little?" That did it. To make my point as definitely as possible, I picked up the glass of water from the coffee table and poured it on his head. "Good night," I said between clenched teeth, "and good-bye!" I stormed up the stairs, tears pouring down my cheeks.

Chapter Ten

"Gee, what happened to you?" Judy asked the next morning. "You look terrible!"

"Thanks, Judy. I can always count on you to make me feel better." I heaved my backpack farther up on my shoulder. "Let's not just stand here, okay? I don't want to be late for school."

She trotted after me across our lawn and onto the sidewalk. "Are you sick or something?"

"Or something," I said.

"So what is it?"

I glanced at her. "Do you mind if we don't talk? I've got a lot on my mind."

"Okay." We trudged along in silence, a

wind that felt like winter whipping at our heels. "Cold, isn't it?" she said after a little while.

I didn't answer. I just didn't trust myself to say anything because I was sure I'd burst into tears even over the weather. Judy kept staring at me. She was walking beside me and though I was looking straight ahead, out of the corner of my eye I could see her face tilted up at me.

"Cut it out," I said, annoyed.

"What? What am I doing?"

"Looking at me."

"Boy! I can't *talk* to you, I can't *look* at you. Are you sure it's okay if I *walk* with you?"

I was tempted to say no, but I didn't. I didn't because just then the wind died down, the sun came out and made the golden leaves of the maples glow so brightly that they hurt my eyes. So instead I started to cry.

We stood there in the middle of the sidewalk, me crying and Judy patting my shoulder until I could take a breath.

"It's over," I said, sniffling.

"What is?"

"Me and Matt."

Judy was shocked. "Why? How? What happened?"

So I told her. She was very sympathetic, shaking her head and making soothing, clucking noises. But when I got to the part about pouring the glass of water on Matt's head, she said, "You didn't! Say you didn't."

"I did, and he deserved it," I said stubbornly.

"It doesn't matter whether he deserved it or not. Lots of people deserve all kinds of things and don't get them. . . ."

"Matthew Boynton's an insensitive jock and that's *all* he is."

Judy wasn't listening. She kept right on talking. "And other people try to keep their cool."

"Cool? Why should I keep my cool? I was angry and hurt and *humiliated*!"

"But all he said was—" Judy began.

"All he said was that I was a lousy reporter!" I started walking faster this time. Judy had to run to catch up.

"That's not what he said. You just told me what he said."

"But that's what he *meant*."

"How do you know what he meant? You have to go by what a person says. Everything else is guesswork. Tiffany, Matt's always been direct and honest with you, hasn't he?"

"You mean for the five minutes I've known him?" I asked sarcastically.

Judy sighed. "My point is that I can understand your being upset at him—kind of. But you asked for his opinion, didn't you?"

"And I sure got it!"

"Listen to me, will you? You were absolutely unfair to him."

I glared at her. "Hey, whose side are you on, anyway?"

"*Your* side, if you'll listen. You wanted to know what he thought of what you'd written and he told you. He just didn't tell you what you wanted to hear."

"*I'll* say!"

"But he *did not* say you were a lousy reporter. He said the *whole thing*, the tape *and* the narration, was too flattering to him, and that it wasn't the real him. He should know, shouldn't he?"

I wouldn't even look at her. Judy didn't understand. How could she? Neither of us said another word as we joined the crowd of kids trooping up the steps into school.

The whole day was a torment. I was afraid I'd run into Matt somewhere, so I was a nervous wreck. I didn't even go to the cafeteria for lunch—not that I could have eaten anything, anyway.

When school was finally over, Walt and Melanie were waiting for me outside.

"So how does it look, Captain?" Walt said.

"Should we record the narration this afternoon or tonight?" Melanie asked eagerly.

"No," I said.

"No, what?" said Melanie. "No to this afternoon or to tonight? Honestly, Tiffany, it's hard to know what you're talking about sometimes."

"Yeah, Tiffany. What gives?" Walt asked.

Luckily Judy arrived just then because I was ready to throttle someone. She said to Melanie and Walt, "The script's not quite ready yet."

"Oh, rats!" said Melanie. "I'm all ready to go. Well, what did Matt think?"

I didn't know what to say but Judy did. "He's—uh—making some notes."

"How long is it gonna take? We've got to turn it in Friday," Walt said.

"I know, Walt," I said icily. "I've never missed a deadline yet."

"Do you need some help on it? I mean, once you get Matt's notes, do you want to have a conference or something?" Walt asked.

"It's a big responsibility. You shouldn't have to do it all yourself."

"Yeah," said Melanie. "Could we help?"

I was surprised at how quickly my annoyance evaporated when they said that. It reminded me that we were all in this thing together. "No, but thanks," I said, forcing a smile. "I'll take care of it."

"Tomorrow then?" Walt asked.

I said, "Right. Tomorrow we'll record Melanie."

As Judy and I walked home, I told her there was no reason why we couldn't have done the recording that day or that night, but she shook her head. "You're in no shape."

I had to agree. "Yeah. But I don't think my shape will be any different tomorrow."

"Don't worry about it. Don't even think about it. Just try to relax tonight," was her advice.

"Fat chance!"

Just as we were finishing dinner at the kitchen table, the front doorbell rang.

"Who could that be?" Mom asked. She looked at me archly. "Are you expecting that nice boy, Tiffany?"

"No, Mother. I'm definitely not—or anyone else."

"Well, would you please see who it is, honey?" Dad said to me.

I didn't want to go to the door just in case it *was* Matt. Not that I expected him to be there—why would he be?—but still, I didn't want to answer the door.

"Tiffany?" Dad said, more loudly this time.

"Okay, okay, I'm going," I said. I got up from the table and went to the front door. Slowly. Really slowly, dragging every step, though as I said, I was sure it wouldn't be Matt.

Chapter Eleven

It wasn't. It was Judy. She bounced in and went directly to the kitchen. My parents were glad to see her—they always were. By the time I got there, she was already digging into a slice of Mom's banana-nut cake.

"Mrs. Welles, you are absolutely the best dessert maker in town," Judy said between mouthfuls.

"What, aside from dessert, brings you here tonight, Judy?" Dad asked.

Judy said, "I've got a problem with my homework, and I thought instead of asking Tiff to help me on the phone I'd . . ."

"Kill two birds with one cake?" Dad joked.

Judy offered to help me do the dishes. When we were finished and were going up to my room, she said, "I really came because I felt bad about how bad you were feeling. And I'm *not* on Matt's side."

I sighed. "Thanks. But that doesn't make me feel any better."

"Yeah, I know. But a little company and a lot of talk might help."

"Maybe."

So we talked. Unfortunately, it didn't help. I was still miserable.

"He hasn't called or anything?" Judy asked.

"Nothing. And if he did, what would I say to him? I really am mad, you know, Judy. After all, I worked very hard on that script. He should have been more aware of how I'd feel. And anyway, I don't care."

"Yes, you do."

"No, I don't."

"Do."

"Don't."

"Do."

We both started to giggle. "You should have seen his face when I poured the water on him," I said.

"Surprised, huh?"

"Well, he sure wasn't expecting it."

"I bet you're the first girl who ever did anything like that to him," Judy said. "The first one who ever dared."

"Yeah. That big, overinflated, twenty-first century Superman!" Suddenly I began to feel a little better. "Our romance may be over, but Matt's going to remember me."

"Right!" said Judy. "That's the way to look at it. Even if he never speaks to you again, you'll be the one girl he'll never forget."

And then I didn't feel better anymore.

Soon Judy had to leave. It was getting late and we both had homework to do. "Oh," she said, "I almost forgot. This was in the letter basket on the front door when I arrived."

She took a small package out of the pocket of her jacket and handed it over. It was addressed to me in a handwriting I didn't recognize. Printed on it in capital letters were the words: PLAY ME.

After she went home, I unwrapped it. It was a videocassette. I figured it was an extra one from Walt. After I finished studying for my chemistry quiz, I went down to the basement to check it out in case it was something important.

It *was* important, but it *wasn't* from Walt.

I sat and watched it on the VCR, entranced.

It was all the stuff we'd cut out of the videos of Matt! All the awkward stuff—the tripping and the falling down at the game, the football hitting him in the head, the fight in the leaves, stuff that had happened at the Bin—all the silly things that make people laugh when they happen to somebody else.

Matt had written narration to go with the tape, making fun of himself, pointing out why he fell here, dropped the dishes there, stepped on a teammate's foot, or ran into the coaches' table. It was as funny as any Woody Allen film I've ever seen, and I laughed so loud that my parents opened the door of the basement and called down to find out what TV show I was watching.

I told them it wasn't a TV show—it was the world's funniest home video. And then I went back to watching Matt make a fool of himself in every possible way.

Near the end of the narration, he had written, "Tiffany, what you're watching is the way I really am a lot of the time. Sometimes I'm also a big jerk. Please don't be mad at me for being a jerk—I'm only human and I make mistakes. I'm sorry I laughed at what you wrote. I think you're a wonderful writer and reporter. I think you're wonderful, period. We don't see things the same way all the time—no two people can—but that's okay as long as we don't take ourselves too seriously. Hey, I'm not mad at you for laughing at me right now!"

When the tape ended, I sat there for a long time, lost in thought.

"You look awful," Judy told me as we walked to school the next morning.

Keeping a straight face, I said, "Thanks, pal. No wonder, considering I was up all night."

"I'm sorry you're still so upset," she said. "No guy's worth it. Take it from me, you'll get over it."

"Thanks again, but I don't intend to."

"Oh, c'mon, Tiff. What're you gonna do, mourn for the rest of your life?"

I glanced at her. "Who said I was mourning?"

"You said you didn't sleep, and—"

"But I didn't say *why* I didn't sleep."

Judy gave me her famous wide-eyed look. "Okay, I'll bite. If it wasn't because of Matt, why didn't you sleep?"

Suppressing a smile, I said, "Because of Matt!" I started walking faster.

"Tiff, stop trying to be mysterious!" she called after me.

I waited for her. "First, I'm mournful, then I'm mysterious. What next?"

Judy eyed me closely. "Actually, you're kind of cheerful. What's going on?"

"Well, the mystery will be solved in my basement today at five o'clock sharp," I told her. "Don't be late!"

Her wail of "Tiffany!" followed me as I broke into a jog, leaving her behind.

I looked for Matt between every one of my classes. But you know how it is—when you want to avoid someone, you usually run into him, and when you really want to run into someone . . . or was he avoiding me? Should I have called him last night after I watched the tape he'd left for me? Had he been expecting me to? And since I didn't, was it now really over between us? Finished? I looked everywhere for him, going hot and cold every time I saw a tall guy with dark hair, but it was never Matt.

Just before last period, I was digging into my locker trying to extract a new notebook—very carefully, I might add. I had no intention of being snagged again.

"From what I can see from the rear," said Matt's wonderful, deep voice, "it's Tiffany Welles—or some of her."

My heart was pounding so hard that I couldn't say a word.

"Are you talking to me yet?" Matt asked. "If not, I'm going to close the door on you and you'll be doomed to spend the rest of your life as a prisoner!"

"Matt! Don't you dare," I yelped, emerging from the locker as fast as I could.

"Do you forgive me?" Matt asked softly. The warning bell for the last class sounded. We were standing there looking at each other, me all flushed from the misery my thoughts had been giving me all day and feeling stupid. Matt looked a little funny, too.

I took a deep breath and said, "Thanks for the tape. If I forgive you, will you forgive me?"

"Of course," he said. "But what do I have to forgive you for?"

"Have you forgotten the shower I gave you?"

"Oh, that!" He laughed. "I guess maybe I deserved it."

Shaking my head, I said, "No, you didn't.

You were only telling me what you thought, which was what I asked you to do."

Matt looked thoughtful. "Yes, you could say that. But there are ways to give someone your opinion that aren't hurtful, right?"

"Right." Then I added, "And there are ways to let someone know you're angry without resorting to mayhem, right?"

"Right." He smiled at me and moved closer. "And now that we've got that settled, I think it's time to kiss and make up, right?"

"Right!" I whispered as his arms went around me and he pressed his lips to mine. It was a long, sweet, wonderful kiss, and it would probably have been even longer if the final bell hadn't rung just then. As we parted and raced down the hall to our classrooms, I said, "Could you come over to my house this afternoon after you're finished at the Bin? The group's gonna be there and I want you to be, too."

"Why? What's up?" Matt asked.

I grinned. "You'll find out when you get there!"

At 4:45 I was pacing in the downstairs hall. The basement was neater than it had ever been. I'd vacuumed and straightened it up, and set out soda, and oatmeal cookies.

I'd even made some caramel corn. Everything was ready. Where was everybody?

When the doorbell finally rang, I opened the door to find Walt and Melanie standing there. Walt was holding a bouquet of flowers.

"What are these for?" I asked as he handed me the bouquet.

"For writing what we know is gonna win us an *A*," Melanie said.

"And for letting Melanie do the narrating," Walt added. "The crew of the *Enterprise* thanks you."

"But you haven't heard it yet," I said as they headed for the basement.

"We're not worried," Melanie said. "I mean, you're a real brain, Tiffany. There's no way you could foul it up."

Then Judy arrived, also with flowers. "They're for you," she said, "because you're being so brave even though your heart is breaking."

"Thanks," I said, trying to look both heartbroken and brave at the same time. "I'd better put them in water."

Judy followed me to the kitchen. "Are Walt and Melanie here yet?" she asked. I nodded. "Then what are we waiting for?"

Just then the doorbell rang. "You'll see," I said, running to answer it.

It was Matt, and he had brought me flowers, too. When Judy saw him, her mouth fell open. But to her credit, nothing came out.

"Oh, you shouldn't have," I whispered, all starry-eyed.

"I didn't. They're for your mother, for letting us use the basement and for all the food." He grinned and so did I.

Then Matt, Judy, and I went downstairs. I announced that I wanted everybody to watch the tape while I read the narration, and then we'd record Melanie reading it. They all said, "Fine," and dug into the food while I turned on the VCR and started to read.

When it was over, I looked up from my script and around the room. There was caramel corn all over the floor. That was the first thing I saw.

The next was a heap of bodies. All four of them were collapsed on the couch, laughing.

"Well?" I said.

Walt spoke first. "It's terrific!"

"Great!" Judy said.

"An *A* for sure," said Melanie.

Matt took my hand and kissed it. "That's my girl," he said.

And then they all started laughing again, and talking. What I'd done, you see, was to incorporate a lot of the awkward, funny moments on the tape with the more serious ones by editing them together. If Walt could do it, I figured, I could, too. When he had explained how we could edit the tape using two VCRs, I had listened very closely although at the time I hadn't even considered doing it myself. Then after I'd viewed the tape Matt had made for me, I'd asked my father the troubleshooter to give me a hand. Using our two VCRs, he had helped me put the two tapes together.

I'd also rewritten my original script because I'd realized that Matt was right. I'd made him into some kind of superhero when he was actually just a very special human being—to me, at least—which was wonderful enough.

That's what I'd been thinking about after I watched the tape he'd left the night before, and that's why I was up all night. After all, we had a deadline to meet, and I wasn't about to let anyone down.

Walt said, "Boy, Tiffany, am I glad you changed the tape we'd made. It would've been dull as a Klingon's brain!"

"Yeah," said Melanie. "You really know how to report reality and make it funny, too!"

Judy hugged me and said, "You sure do!" And then she whispered, "I'm gonna get you for not telling me about you and Matt being back together!"

When everyone had finally quieted down, we recorded Melanie reading the new narration, and she did a very good job.

After supper that evening, I was washing the dishes. Mom was on the phone, and Dad was reading the paper when the doorbell rang.

"Who would it be this time, Tiffany?" Dad asked from the depths of the sports section.

"Oh, that would be Matt," I said, beaming.

And it was.

So that's what happened to me a little over a year ago. It's November, and I'm a senior now. Matt's a freshman at C.U., but he's home almost every weekend, and we double-date a lot with Judy and Roger. Incidentally, our group got an *A* for our report, and it was shown to great acclaim and laughter at the awards assembly. I used the report—with credit given to the rest of the group, of course—as my application for the internship at the *Bugle*, and I got it! I've been working there after school three days a week, and it's really great!

I guess I'm pretty lucky. I got what I had been wishing for—a wonderful boyfriend and a wonderful job. But I had to change the way I looked at the world before my wishes could come true. It wasn't exactly easy, but you know what? It wasn't really all that hard!